"If my mother has something wrong with her heart, I need to know—whether she likes it or not," Ian said.

"Worried?"

Sure he was worried. Worse than worried. "Mom has been my rock for a long time. Now I have to be hers."

With the whisper-touch of her fingers, Gretchen stopped Ian's nervous jiggling of his straw. "Would you like some company?"

Ian studied her sincere expression, a dozen conflicting emotions going off in his head. "Are you offering?"

"I am."

He knew he should refuse, but he wanted her company. "I'd like that."

Boy, was he in trouble. The woman had him in a tangle. He wanted to know her better.

And he wasn't sure what to do about it.

Books by Linda Goodnight

Love Inspired

In the Spirit of...Christmas #326
A Very Special Delivery #349
**A Season for Grace* #377
**A Touch of Grace* #390

**The Brothers' Bond*

LINDA GOODNIGHT

A romantic at heart, Linda Goodnight believes in the traditional values of family and home. Writing books enables her to share her certainty that, with faith and perseverance, love can last forever and happy endings really are possible.

A native of Oklahoma, Linda lives in the country with her husband, Gene, and Mugsy, an adorably obnoxious rat terrier. She and Gene have a blended family of six grown children. An elementary school teacher, she is also a licensed nurse. When time permits, Linda loves to read, watch football and rodeo, and indulge in chocolate. She also enjoys taking long, calorie-burning walks in the nearby woods. Readers can write to her at linda@lindagoodnight.com, or c/o Steeple Hill Books, 233 Broadway, Suite 1001, New York, NY 10279.

A Touch of Grace

Linda Goodnight

Published by Steeple Hill Books™

STEEPLE HILL BOOKS

ISBN-13: 978-0-373-87426-2
ISBN-10: 0-373-87426-X

A TOUCH OF GRACE

This edition published by arrangement with Steeple Hill Books.

www.SteepleHill.com

Printed in U.S.A.

Is not this the kind of fasting I have chosen?...Is it not to share your food with the hungry and to provide the poor wanderer with shelter? When you see the naked to clothe him, and not to turn away from your own flesh and blood?...Then you will call and the Lord will answer, you will cry for help, and he will say: Here am I.

—*Isaiah* 58:6–7, 9

This book is dedicated to adoptive parents everywhere. You are God's word in action.

Prologue

Ian couldn't stop shaking. He'd done something bad. Real bad. And now they were all in trouble.

Collin always said you shouldn't tell nobody nothing. But he and his brothers had been cold. That's why Drew made the fire, but Ian's prekindergarten teacher didn't understand. Her eyes got all watery and she took him to the school counselor. Ian hadn't said nothing to Mr. James. He'd been too scared. But Ms. Smith told everything. Even stuff Ian didn't say. Stuff about hi-jean and neglect and other words he didn't know.

Now all three brothers were in the office. Him and Drew and Collin.

He looked across the cluttered room to where Collin stood with fists tight at his side. He hoped Collin wasn't mad at him for telling.

Collin was ten, the big brother. He took care of Ian and Drew. Collin was brave. He didn't even get scared when it thundered and rain slithered through the cracks of the trailer like wet snakes. He didn't get scared neither when the cops came. He told them Mama was at the store and would be right back. But that wasn't true. Sometimes Mama didn't come back for days and days.

Drew leaped up from the plastic chair and charged for the door. "Leave me alone!"

Ian jumped at the sudden outburst.

"I'm not going this time. You can't make me."

Ian's belly started to hurt. He sneaked a glance at Collin. Collin didn't like it when Drew freaked out. That's what Collin called it. Freakin' out. Drew was mad, kicking and spitting and screaming. Bad stuff happened when Drew freaked out.

Sure enough, Mr. James grabbed his brother and pushed him into a chair. Mr. James was nice, but he was strong. With big muscles. And Drew was only seven.

"Settle down. Right now," Mr. James said. "We're trying to help."

Drew struggled, growling like a mean tomcat. His too-long brown hair flopped wildly. He spit at Mr. James and said a bad word. Now he'd be in worse trouble. Drew never knew when to stop.

Ian couldn't help it then. He started to cry. He clamped his lips tight and tried to stop, but he couldn't. The sound stuck inside him, like peanut butter swallowed too fast. His chest hurt. He didn't want the counselor to be mad at him, too. He didn't want anyone to be mad. But he was scared and the tears pushed hard at the backs of his eyes.

His legs shook so much his hand-me-down tennis shoes nearly fell off.

He looked at Collin, afraid to talk for fear he'd say the wrong thing again. He needed to go the bathroom but wasn't about to ask. What if the social worker took him away this time, and he never got to see Drew and Collin again? Mama said that would happen if they went around shooting off at the mouth.

He shouldn't have told.

The tears ran through his nose and into the corners of his lips. He swiped at his face with the buttonless sleeve of his flannel shirt. This was all his fault.

Then Collin came over and put a hand on his head. Not a mad hand. A gentle, don't-cry, hand. A quivery sigh ran through Ian. Collin would take care of him. He always did.

The social worker lady came over, too, and squatted down in front of his chair. She had nice eyes. And her voice was soft like Ms. Smith's. But Collin didn't like her. Ian could tell. Collin's face was hard and mad, kind of scary.

"Don't cry, Ian. I know you're upset," the lady said. "But you're going to a real nice place that's warm and has plenty to eat."

Ian sniffed and looked at the woman. She smelled so nice. Much better than Mama. But he loved Mama. He wished she'd come home.

The social worker tapped the end of his shoe. The old stringless thing slipped off his heel. "We'll get you some new tennis shoes, too. Ones that fit."

Ian sucked in a hiccup. Shoes that fit. He'd like that. These were cold. The bottoms had holes and the inside was torn out. Sometimes they made sore places.

He wondered if he'd get some socks, too. White ones

that came high up his leg and didn't fall down when he walked.

He hoped they went back to the same foster house again. The lady there was soft and smiley and let him eat all the food he wanted. He didn't know why Collin and Drew didn't like foster houses.

"Collin." The social worker looked up at his big brother. "You're old enough to understand that this is for the best. You boys can't continue living alone in that old trailer. Now, why don't you help us get the little ones into the car?"

Collin didn't even look at her. He stared at the wall like a superhero trying to look through to the other side.

Mr. James did a funny thing then. Keeping one hand on Drew's shoulder, he got down on his knees in front of the chair and talked about baseball and God.

He said, "Boys, sometimes life throws a curveball. But remember, no matter what happens today or forever, Jesus will always be with you, watching over you."

Collin must be a lot like Jesus. He always watched over Drew and Ian when Mama was gone. Well, even when Mama was home.

Then Mr. James bowed his head and started whispering. A prayer, Ian thought. The room got real quiet. Even Drew quit fighting.

When the prayer ended, Mr. James handed them each a little key chain with a metal fish on it. Collin wouldn't take his.

"This is a gift from me to you, not as your counselor, but as a friend who cares." He stared up at the social worker as if daring her to argue. She looked at the door and didn't say a thing. "You don't have to take it, Collin, but I hope you will. It's a reminder that God will always care for you no matter where you go or what you do. He'll never leave you. Never."

Ian liked the sound of that. Jesus must be real nice.

Even though he stood stiff as a statue, Collin let Mr. James put the key chain in his hand. He wanted it. He was just too mad to say so. Then his voice scraped the air like rusty metal. "Where we going this time?"

The social worker lady stood up and moved toward him like she might touch him. Collin backed away.

"We've found placements for Drew and Ian."

Ian's heart slammed against his rib cage. What about Collin? He didn't go anywhere without Collin.

"Together?" Collin asked.

"Not this time. I'm sorry."

What was she saying? That he and his brothers wouldn't be together? That he would be all by himself with a bunch of strange people? His legs started jerking again.

"They stay with me," Collin said, but this time he sounded uncertain, as if maybe something bad was about to happen and he couldn't fix it. "Ian gets scared at night."

The lady touched Collin's arm and her voice went soft and sweet. "He'll be fine. They both will be. And so will you. Now, come on. We need to go."

Turning, she held out her hand to Ian and smiled. He looked at Collin, saw the truth in his big brother's eyes. This time Mama was right. Collin and Drew would go away and leave him. He would never see his brothers again. All because of his big fat mouth.

Chapter One

Twenty-three years later, New Orleans

"Dead!"

Head still foggy from a nightmarish sleep, Ian Carpenter pushed up on one elbow. He tried to shake himself awake enough to think straight. Someone had discovered a dead girl on the grounds of Isaiah House.

Heart jump-started by the horror of such a thing, he squinted one eye at the red digital alarm clock. Six-fifteen. After combing the streets of the French Quarter most of the night, he'd been in bed less than three hours. Whatever happened had gone down in that brief time.

Sometimes the futility of what he did was overwhelming.

Through a throat filled with gravel, he said, "I'll be right down."

In five minutes flat, he had showered and dressed in his usual jeans and T-shirt. He shoved on the new pair of Nike Shox he'd purchased yesterday, finding little joy in them now, and tiptoed down the squeaky wooden stairs of the old three-story mission house. Soon enough, the ten in-house residents would begin the day and he would be expected in the chapel with a word or to play the saxophone.

Ian both loved and hated his calling. He loved the people. He loved ministering and counseling. And he especially loved when someone's life was turned around by the power of God's love. But he hated times like these when the dark side won.

In the predawn September morning, he opened the back door out into the courtyard, a beautiful, lush green sanctuary where he often prayed and sought answers to the myriad problems of Isaiah House, the mission he'd started three years ago on faith and a few hundred dollars.

God had called him to this place of beauty and debauchery before Hurricane Katrina. Since the disaster, his work had more than tripled. Originally a small haven for runaways, Isaiah House now did whatever it could for any and everyone. True to the scripture that served as its cornerstone, the mission was a hand extended to whoever needed it. Sometimes that hand was stretched pretty thin.

This morning his courtyard sanctuary was hushed, the willows weeping condensation onto the cobblestone walkway as if mourning what lay just outside the mission walls. Beyond the dripping-wet elephant ears and lemon-scented magnolias, yellow police tape vibrated in the twilight stillness.

The stark contrast wasn't lost on Ian. He'd worked

the streets and slums of various cities all over the country since junior high school when Mom and Dad signed him up for summer missions' work. Now, at twenty-eight, he'd come to understand all too well that beauty and tragedy coexisted everywhere. Sometimes he felt overwhelmed by his need to make a difference and the utter numbers of despairing mankind.

Ian leaned for a second against the rough bark of a moss-draped oak and squeezed his sleep-gritty eyes shut against the covered body lying on the ground.

Somebody had lost a loved one.

He hadn't even heard the sirens. No surprise. They went on all night in this part of New Orleans. Sirens and reveling. And the desperate meanderings of runaways and drug addicts.

"Grace for today, Father," he said simply. "To do Your work."

And as always peace descended. He pushed off the giant oak, opened the lacy black iron gate and walked toward the buzzing hive of police activity inside the yellow tape.

"You the reverend?" an ebony-faced policeman, dressed in city blues, asked.

"Yes, I'm Ian Carpenter." He had never been comfortable with the formalities of his profession. He was a street missionary, plain and simple. As his mama liked to say, "There but for the grace of God go you or I." He was no better or more holy than anyone else. Reverend might fit some, but not him.

"What happened?"

"Looks like an overdose." Even in the early morning,

with the sun only peeking above the horizon, sweat beaded the officer's forehead. Death was hard work for anyone. "You think she was comin' to your place?"

"Possibly."

"You mind having a look, see if you know her?"

Ian glanced toward the plastic-draped body. Unfortunately, in his line of work, this wouldn't be a first. If she was a local, chances were pretty good that he'd at least seen her before. The street people were his love and his life. He made it a point to know them.

"Okay." Though he dreaded what was to come, he fell in step with the officer and walked the few yards to the body.

With a respect Ian appreciated, the cop gently pulled the plastic away from a young woman's deathly white face. Ian's heart fell to his knees. A weight as heavy as the humidity over Lake Pontchartrain pressed against his lungs.

Maddy. Lost forever. So close to the help here in the mission that he and God longed to offer. Yet, she hadn't made it.

Another failure for Ian.

He rubbed the back of his neck and blew out a weary sigh. He'd had the dream again last night. The nightmare where he was trapped in a dark place, filthy and cold and scared. For once, he hadn't minded the phone yanking him from his bed. Not until he'd discovered the reason.

"Her name is Maddy," he said quietly. "She stayed here for a couple of weeks."

And for a while Ian had hoped she would heal. But no matter how much he'd prayed and counseled, one day she'd walked out, back to the addiction that had finally stolen her life. She'd once been beautiful, a curse on the streets, but a way to pay for the drugs. So young. And her big green eyes were always filled with confusion.

The officer jotted the information onto a tiny spiral notebook, then squinted up at him. "You know her last name?"

"No." Most of the time, street people didn't share identifying information and he accepted them as they came. "But she was a sweet kid. Gentle. Kind of innocent, if that makes sense. Innocent and lost."

"Any kin you know of? Family she might have mentioned?"

Ian shook his head, feeling worse by the minute. He'd tried to minister to Maddy's soul, but he didn't know much about her former life. Every time he'd asked, she'd walked away. "I'll ask around."

Some of Isaiah House's other residents might have known her better than he had.

A blue Channel Eleven News van careened to a stop along the edge of the street and a petite woman jumped out.

Ian groaned inwardly.

Just what he didn't need this morning. Gretchen Barker, the Channel Eleven barracuda. An investigative reporter with a reputation as a watchdog for the public, Gretchen's particular interest of late was religious groups. For the last year and a half she'd had her nose and camera in every New Orleans charity, making sure they toed the line.

Ian had no problem with that. He strongly believed

that churches and charitable organizations should be held accountable for every donated penny. But he did have trouble with the woman's attitude. Though he ran a squeaky-clean organization, Isaiah House had come under her scrutiny and her criticism a couple of times lately for the most mundane things.

She seemed especially interested in Ian's finances, which was ludicrous to say the least. Every month Ian waited, partly in fear and partly in anticipation to see how God would keep Isaiah House afloat. As for his personal accounts, he wasn't exactly stockpiling luxury cars and vacation houses. He lived in the mission and drove an old passenger van that needed an overhaul. His only indulgence was on his feet.

"We don't need any reporters out here yet." The officer eyed the van with similar distaste. "This poor girl may be dead but she deserves some respect."

Ian had to agree. "I'll go talk to them."

By now, Barracuda Barker was standing at the yellow tape, straining toward the body on the ground as the police officer repositioned the plastic before carefully covering the victim's face.

Before anyone could stop her, the reporter grabbed the tape and slid beneath.

"Whoa, lady." Ian hurried toward her. The police had yet to finish their investigation and the forensic crew had only just arrived. "You can't come past that tape."

Face set, Gretchen Barker pushed by him. Ian caught her arm. "Did you hear me?"

The reporter's head swiveled toward him. Beneath

hair the color of gold, her face was pale. She yanked from his grip and started to run toward the still form on the ground. Ian caught her from behind, wrapping both arms around her waist. She kicked out, caught his left shin with the sharp heel of her sandal. Ian yelped, but held on. He'd never seen a reporter act so bizarre. She couldn't want the story that badly.

He looked toward the photojournalist on the opposite side of the tape. The cameraman stood stock-still, staring at the scene, clearly shocked at the behavior of his colleague.

In that brief instant while Ian looked at the cameraman, the barracuda slammed an elbow into his lax gut. "Let me go. I need to see."

Air whooshed out of him. He loosened his grip, but not before she whirled around and slammed the heel of her hand beneath his chin, knocking his teeth painfully together. Ian's head popped backward. For a little woman, she packed a wallop.

What was her problem anyway? Was she so bent on getting her story that she had no respect for the dead? The idea curled Ian's hair.

He caught her arm before she could slam him again. This time he stared fully into her face. What he saw gave him pause. Something was seriously wrong here.

Fear, not determination, dilated her pupils.

Ian relented a little. The death of someone so young was a hard thing to deal with—even for him.

Had she never reported a death scene before?

If that was her trouble, she deserved his understanding. Even though he choked a little to think of the barracuda and compassion in the same sentence, Ian tried one more time.

"Gretchen," he said. "You know better than to break the police barrier. What's wrong? How can I help? Haven't you ever reported a death scene before?"

Her chest rose and fell. Her entire body trembled. Her mouth worked but nothing came out. And then, with an anguished cry that Ian would remember as long as he lived, she looked toward the body on the ground and said, "That's my sister!"

Ian looked from the huge green eyes of the reporter to the covered body of the dead girl. Huge green eyes. They had the same eyes.

He had been breathless before, but now he couldn't breathe at all. This strong, self-confident woman was a sister to fragile, helpless Maddy?

"Maddy. Maddy." And then the woman he'd considered tough and hardened shattered before his eyes. She went to her knees on the thick, wet grass and sobbed brokenly. Ian followed her down, guilty for the negative thoughts he'd had about her, and gathered the shaking Gretchen to his chest.

"I'm sorry, so sorry," he muttered against silky hair that smelled as fresh as the flowers in his garden.

Gretchen Barker, the barracuda whose news reports had teeth in them, felt small and soft and helpless in his arms. A protective urge, totally out of place given who she was, suffused Ian. For a man who kept women at arm's length to protect the integrity of the mission, having a beautiful, grief-stricken woman in his embrace was not an everyday occurrence.

If he hadn't been so saddened by the circumstances, Ian would have seen the humor in his predicament. He didn't even like the thorn-in-the-flesh reporter and here he was thinking how pretty she was and how good her hair smelled. He was more than exhausted. He was losing his mind.

Reining in the wayward thoughts, he gently patted her back until the racking sobs subsided. Slowly, she pulled away, leaving damp spots on his green T-shirt. Her bereft expression tore at him.

"Could I call someone for you? A friend? Your family?"

"Maddy is my family." Her face crumpled. She pressed shaking fingertips against her lips. "Oh, Maddy."

Wanting to help, but not certain what to expect from a woman who'd kicked him, hit him and then collapsed in tears, he slipped his arm around her narrow shoulders. For a fraction of a second, she relented and leaned against his side. Then, she placed a hand on his shoulder and pushed up. The knees of her dark slacks were grass-stained and soaked with dew.

Crossing her arms as if they could shield her heart from the terrible sorrow, she said, "I have to see her."

Ian understood. He didn't like it, but he understood. "I'll ask the officer."

Since she was next of kin, they had no problem securing permission. The police appreciated a positive ID.

Slowly, they walked toward the body. Ian had never in his life wanted so badly to comfort someone. She was shattered. She needed another human being to help her through this, but now that she'd gathered her composure and made up her mind to see her sister, she had pulled away from him, both emotionally and physically. She tolerated his presence, but not his comfort.

She knelt beside her sister's body and waited for the policeman.

The officer's dark, rough hand rustled the plastic. "Are you ready, ma'am?"

Shoulders stiff and resolute, she gave one curt nod.

When the still face was revealed, Gretchen didn't react. She knelt there, staring down for the longest time. At last, when Ian wondered if perhaps there had been some mistake and this wasn't her sister after all, she nodded.

"That's Maddy."

The policeman slid the cover back in place and moved quietly away, leaving them alone. Gretchen still didn't move.

Another siren wailed in the distance. Across the street teenagers bounced a basketball while staring openly at the swarming police, trying to get a peek at the tragedy. Motors roared. Doors slammed. Voices carried on the morning air. Other news crews had arrived by now and were filming from outside the barrier.

Regardless of her occupation, Ian wanted to get Gretchen away from the reporters.

"Tell me what you need, Gretchen. What can I do?" Ian asked.

"Do?" she asked. "Do?"

She shot up from her knees, and that quick the barracuda returned. She turned on him, green eyes flashing fire. "I think you've done enough."

He had no idea what she meant, but the lady was distraught.

He reached for her. “Gretchen.”

She slapped his hands away, striking out like a wounded animal. “You don’t know me.”

Ignoring the rejection, he offered his hand again, palm up. He couldn’t leave her like this. “You need to get away from here. Come on, I’ll take you inside the mission.”

“Oh, you’d like that, wouldn’t you? Take me inside and feed me soup and a pack of lies. Tell me that you have all the answers to my problems like you did for my poor druggie sister.” Her face contorted in sarcasm. “You were different, Maddy said. You could help her get her life together.” She glanced from her sister’s still form to Ian, stabbing him with accusing green eyes. “Well, you really did a good job of that, didn’t you?”

While Ian grappled to understand why he was the focus of her animosity, Gretchen Barker, the Channel Eleven barracuda, stormed across the wet grass to her van and drove away.

Chapter Two

The long, slow notes of "Amazing Grace" reverberated on the air and trembled into silence. Even in the worst of times, Ian found solace in his music and in the beautiful old saxophone his father had given him. Like the Psalmist David, he felt closer to God when he played than when he prayed.

He leaned the instrument carefully against a chair and went to answer the knock on his office door.

The bushy, gray mustache of Roger Bryant twitched at him from the doorway. "You fretting about something, son?"

Roger always knew when something was eating at him. He claimed the saxophone sounded different. Ian figured it was true enough. Through his music he was able to express the emotions that otherwise stayed locked inside.

Roger, skinny and frail with scraggly strands of gray hair slicked down with some kind of shiny oil, was one of Ian's first success stories. At fifty-nine, his ash-gray face and broken body looked seventy, a testament to years of slavery to alcohol and self-loathing. Homeless and destitute after too many stints in county lockup, he'd asked Ian to help him get his life together. Then he'd stuck around to help run Isaiah House. For Ian, who loved the hands-on part of ministry but detested the business end, Roger had literally been an answer to prayer.

"I just got off the phone with our lawyer," he said to his friend.

Roger, hampered by a hip badly in need of replacement, limped into the office. His basset-hound face showed little reaction to Ian's statement. He wasn't shaken by much. "Bad news, I guess?"

Ian tilted his head in agreement. "The lawsuit will likely go to trial." He'd thought the whole thing a joke at first.

"Foolishness. Who would expect a Christian mission to allow pornographic magazines on-site?"

"That's my thinking. But even if a jury agrees, it will cost us a lot of money. And the mission can't afford that right now." Donations were down this summer for some reason while the need increased.

"Want to know what I think?" Roger propped his bad hip against the edge of a desk littered with papers, files and orange soda cans.

"You're going to tell me anyway."

Roger grinned. Even then, his face looked soulful. "I think that lady politician is at the bottom of this somewhere."

"Marian Jacobs?" Ian rubbed at the knot forming

along the top of his right shoulder. The mission had plenty of naysayers who would like to see it closed, or at least, moved elsewhere. Runaways and street kids were a blight on the thriving tourist industry and any number of nearby businesses wanted them gone. Marian Jacobs happened to be one of the more influential.

"Yeah. Her. She wants to shut us down real bad."

Last winter, the city councilwoman had enforced some ridiculous zoning ordinance that kept him from setting up cots in the chapel on the coldest nights. Before that she'd complained long and hard about the negative impact Isaiah House had on the happy-go-lucky atmosphere of the tourist district. Her post-Katrina revitalization for the city did not include street people or the ministries designed to help them.

"She doesn't like me much, that's for sure." Outside his office window three bright red cardinals pecked at sunflower seeds sprinkled beneath a willow. "Your birds are about out of feed."

Roger doted on the birds, just as he did on the equally flighty runaways who landed at Isaiah House.

"You going to Maddy's funeral?" Leave it to Roger to cut to the chase.

With all the other worries on his mind, the last thing Ian wanted to do on a hot, humid Friday afternoon was attend a funeral.

"Sometimes being a minister stinks." Most people would be shocked to hear him say such a thing. His mother for one. But not Roger. His placid face, lined and furrowed, never seemed shaken by anything Ian blurted out. He was about the only person Ian could share his frustrations and worries with.

Ministers were always expected to do the right thing, even when it hurt. Ian wasn't perfect but he didn't like to disappoint anyone, either. He worked hard to avoid that feeling. Somehow he worried about alienating the people around him.

His hand snaked into his pocket, found the familiar key chain and took it out. He'd had the thing forever, though he wasn't even certain where it had come from. Maybe his parents had given it to him the time he'd been in the hospital with meningitis. He wasn't sure, but he was certain that he'd been terrified then of being alone. Every time Mom and Dad had left the room, he'd thought they wouldn't come back. So, he figured that's when they'd given him the little fish that said, "I will never leave you nor forsake you."

Wherever the key chain had come from, the words never failed to comfort him.

Funny that he would think of that now.

"God called me to heal the brokenhearted, to set the captive free," he said, paraphrasing his favorite verses from Isaiah. "Maddy was both. I didn't do enough."

Roger clamped a bony hand on his shoulder. "How many times have you talked about free will, Ian? Maddy made her own decisions."

"Yeah. Bad ones." He felt so inadequate at times like this. Wounded souls were his responsibility. That's why he drove the streets for hours each night ministering to runaways and street kids. But nothing he did was ever enough.

"You can't help Maddy, but she's got a sister."

Ian drew in a deep breath then let it go in one gust.

"I was thinking the same thing." Barracuda or not, Gretchen Barker was hurting.

He only hoped seeing her didn't stir up trouble. He had enough of that already.

Gretchen gazed through dark glasses at the small group assembled amidst the sun-bleached tombs and scalding heat of Carter Cemetery. Not many had gathered to pay their last respects to Madeline Michelle Barker. As hard as that was for Gretchen to handle, she understood. Maddy's brief life hadn't made much of a mark.

As the hired minister said the final "amen," Gretchen swallowed back the sobs that seemed to be constantly stuck below her breastbone straining for release.

The small gathering began to scurry away, eager to escape the energy-zapping heat and humidity. Who could blame them?

Gretchen shoved her slippery sunglasses higher, saw that her fingers trembled. Sometimes she got tired of being the strong one.

The moment the thought came, she nearly buckled. Who would she be strong for now?

Less than twenty people, most of them Gretchen's friends and coworkers, had attended the simple graveside services. Even Mom and Dad hadn't come, citing the distance between California and Louisiana. But Gretchen knew the truth. They had long ago washed their hands of the daughter who couldn't get her life together. And so had everyone else. Everyone but Gretchen.

Tears pushed at the back of her eyes, hot and painful. She'd cried so much these past few days, she should be dehydrated. Digging yet another clean tissue from her handbag, she dabbed at her wet cheeks.

Carlotta, her best friend and roommate, rubbed the center of her back. "You okay?"

"No," she said honestly. Carlotta would understand. She knew the number of times Gretchen had taken Maddy into their apartment, given her money, tried to get her clean. Enabler, some people called her. And now she was terrified that they may have been right. Had her desire to protect her sister ultimately caused her death?

Her friend's gorgeous Latina eyes darkened with compassion. "Ready to go home?"

She shook her head, felt her hair stick to the side of her neck. "I want to stay here awhile."

When Carlotta started to argue, Gretchen said, "Go. I'm fine. I just need a little more time."

"The service was nice, Gretchen. Maddy would have liked it."

"Yeah." Regardless of her ambivalence toward religion, she couldn't let Maddy leave this life without some hope that things would be better somewhere else. Life here hadn't been all that good for her sister.

Carlotta hovered for another minute, her concern touching. Finally, she said, "I'll see you later, then? Maybe an hour or so?"

"Sure. Go on. I'm fine." She wasn't fine. She was

splintered in half. Maddy had been the other part of her, and now she was gone.

Carlotta gave her one last hug and turned to leave. After two steps, she stopped, turning back. Voice lowered, she tilted her head toward the rear of the funeral tent.

"I don't know if you noticed, but there's a man still back there that I don't recognize. The nice-looking guy in the blue shirt. Do we know him?"

Carlotta wouldn't leave her alone here in the cemetery with a stranger even if the guy was movie star gorgeous.

Gretchen followed her gaze to the well-built figure, recognizing him immediately.

Ian Carpenter. The mission preacher. She should have known he'd show up.

She sucked in the scent of decaying funeral wreaths. "I don't want him here."

He'd phoned her twice, though she had no idea where he'd gotten her number. Once to offer his services and the chapel for the funeral. Another time to ask if he could do anything to help her. Right. As if she would allow that.

She knew his kind. Smile kindly, talk softly, and lure the lonely and needy into a web of deceit under the guise of religion.

The sad, sick feeling in the pit of her stomach was replaced by a slow-burning anger. He had no right. And anger was easier to bear than raw, scalding grief.

Carlotta gave her a funny look. "Who is he?"

"Ian Carpenter. He runs the mission where Maddy was—" The horrible image of her sister lying lifeless on the dew-drenched grass returned with a vengeance.

She, who could report the most heinous crime or natural disaster with aplomb, couldn't seem to keep her emotions in check this time. She supposed that was normal, though she hated the weakness.

Carlotta gave her hand an encouraging squeeze.

"He must feel awful that she was so close to his mission and he wasn't able to save her."

"I think he feels guilty."

From behind the cover of her shades, Gretchen glared at the preacher. He stood alone beneath the green funeral home canopy, quiet and unobtrusive, one hand in the pocket of his black slacks.

If she'd been in any condition to notice such things, the preacher was easy on the eyes. She'd bet a special report scoop that he put those looks to good use for the cause of his mission.

Medium height. Medium build. Medium brown hair. Everything about him was medium, except for the eyes. They were startling, a brilliant aquamarine made even more dramatic by his blue dress shirt.

Was it those hypnotic eyes that had attracted Maddy?

"Gretchen. Come on," Carlotta chided, her words tinged with both sympathy and exasperation. "Guilty for what? For not knowing Maddy was out there in the middle of the night?"

But Gretchen wasn't ready for simple answers. She wanted to probe deeper.

"Why was she on the mission grounds? Why not inside? She was supposed to be a resident there, getting help, getting clean. But she wasn't. Did someone at

Isaiah House hurt her? Scare her? Cause her to run away again?"

She'd been mulling over the idea for the past two days. Maddy was vulnerable, easily wounded. Someone who liked to play mind games could do a lot of damage. And weren't mind games what religion was about?

"Not every ministry is dirty, Gretchen."

"His is." Gretchen shot Ian one more glare and turned away. "I just know it."

Carlotta sighed and shoved her glossy, black hair over one shoulder. She had an amazing capacity to look cool and fresh in the worst of New Orleans's heat.

"All right, honey. Whatever you think. I'm not going to argue with you today. Are you sure you don't want me to drive you home?"

"No. You go on." Gretchen wasn't quite ready to leave Maddy here alone.

"All right. Call if you need me."

Carlotta left, her long legs moving with grace and speed across the narrow patches of grass to her sporty car. Gretchen refused to think another thought about Ian Carpenter. For all she cared he could roast.

Taking yet another tissue, she approached the mausoleum that held her sister's body. She hadn't wanted to bury Maddy here in a place where tourists prowled the tombs in search of macabre thrills. But she hadn't much choice. California was too far away. And Mom and Dad didn't want her there anyway.

"Oh, Maddy. Why couldn't I help you get over the hurts? Why couldn't you ever heal?" Fragile Maddy had been broken by the same evil that had made Gretchen strong. No one would ever fool her again. She would spend her career ferreting out the wolves in sheep's clothing like Brother Gordon and the Family of Love.

She reached out to touch the white stone. Suddenly, the childhood Maddy was alive and well inside her head. The blond princess in pink ballet slippers. At six, Mama had auditioned her for commercials because she was so pretty. That was when they'd met Brother Gordon. He'd invited them to what he called the common man's Bible study. And none of them was ever the same after that.

She stood there in front of the tomb for a long time, remembering, regretting, wishing for another chance. At one point she glanced back and noticed with relief that Ian Carpenter had disappeared. Good.

She didn't know what to make of him. He'd been kind the day of Maddy's death and she'd been too distraught to see that. She didn't want to be unfair, but she feared men like Ian. Preachers, as she well knew, wielded power over their followers, whether for good or for bad.

Which was Ian Carpenter?

She remembered one of her last conversations with Maddy, two weeks before her death. She'd seemed so full of hope, excited to be attending classes at the mission. Thrilled to see her sister happy, Gretchen hadn't asked what kind of classes, though a cold fear had snaked down her spine that day. She'd warned Maddy to be careful. Had even begged her sister to let her find a more conventional rehab. But Maddy had assured her that Ian Carpenter was the real deal. He could help her get her life together. She would make it this time.

But she hadn't.

Now Gretchen needed to know. What exactly went on inside Isaiah Mission?

The afternoon sun angled from the west casting shadows over the rows and rows of pale tombs. As much as she hated leaving her sister behind, Gretchen was too tired to stay any longer. Carlotta would be calling soon, wondering where she was, if she was all right. And she'd promised to be back at the news station tomorrow morning, bright and early. She desperately needed some sleep.

She leaned her cheek briefly against the vault and whispered, "I love you," and turned to go.

A long human shadow touched her toes.

She jerked her head up.

Ian Carpenter came toward her, a tall soft drink cup in hand. "You look like you could use this."

As parched as she was, Gretchen balked at the idea of taking anything from him. Brother Gordon had been nice at first, too.

A near smile softened the edges of a very nice mouth. "Go ahead. I promise it's only lemonade, not cyanide."

Did he have any idea how *not* funny that was?

She took the cup and drank deeply, the tart citrus cutting the terrible dryness in her throat.

All the while, she watched him over the rim of the cup. His electric eyes held hers, steady and quiet, studying her.

He had a serenity about him that was almost eerie.

"Thank you," she said, after gulping half the supersized drink. "I didn't realize I'd stayed so long."

"It's been a hard day for you."

Gretchen was too uncertain about his motives to answer.

"Maddy was a sweet girl," he went on. "A gentle and kind person."

"And weak." She took another sip of lemonade. The sides of the cup dripped condensation onto her black crepe dress.

"We all have weaknesses."

"Even you, Reverend?"

"Me most of all. And one of my weaknesses is being called Reverend. I prefer Ian." Lightly, he slid a hand under her elbow. "Your nose is getting pink. You need to get out of the sun."

Normally opposed to anyone telling her what to do, Gretchen was too numb and exhausted to resist. She walked with him to an iron bench in a small, shady spot. Her insides trembled with fatigue and emotion. She really should go home.

"My roommate will be worried."

"The woman with you? Tall. Black hair."

She expected him to expound on her roommate's beauty as most men did, but he didn't. He settled onto the bench, keeping a polite distance between them. Gretchen couldn't help but appreciate that.

"Carlotta Moreno. She's a good friend." She shook her head and studied the real slice of lemon floating in her cup. If Maddy had more friends like Carlotta, maybe someone would have been with her that night. "I wish…"

As if he understood the direction of her thoughts, Ian said, "Maddy had friends, too. People who cared about her."

Unable to stop a bitter laugh, she swept her arm around the cemetery. "Oh, yes, the place is brimming with them."

"They were here."

She looked at him, trying to comprehend why he would tell an obvious lie. His startling eyes gazed back at her, steady and quiet.

"Are they invisible?" she asked sarcastically.

"In a manner of speaking."

"Metaphysically speaking, you mean? As in astral projection or some spiritual out-of-body experience?"

He laughed. She was dead serious and he laughed.

"I meant that some of Maddy's friends were here, paying their respects out of sight of the other mourners. They were worried that you'd be upset if they showed themselves."

"Are you telling me that there were people behind the tombs listening to the funeral service?"

"The residents of the mission who knew her and a few street people."

"I don't believe you."

He shrugged. "Come to Isaiah House and ask them yourself."

Gretchen smiled grimly. She should have seen that one coming.

"Maybe I will." But not for the reasons he had in mind.

"We have chapel mornings and evenings at seven. Bible studies are pretty much ongoing, some formal, some informal."

"Or I could come for the soup." The silliness slipped out and she laughed. Then guilt rushed in. How could she laugh on the day of her sister's funeral?

"Laughter is the best medicine, and it's a lot less expensive."

The preacher was uncannily intuitive. She'd better be more careful. "But my sister was buried today."

He grew quiet for a minute, as if he drew inside. Gretchen wondered if he was praying. Elbows to knees, hands clasped together in front of his face, he bounced thumb knuckles against his chin.

"I won't pretend to understand Maddy's death, because I don't. If I was God, she'd still be alive today."

His intense honesty surprised her. He didn't sound like any preacher she'd ever heard before. She had expected platitudes.

"Aren't you going to tell me that Maddy's suffering is over now? Or that she's in a far better place?" Trite little sayings that infuriated her.

He shook his head. A small scar gleamed white through the brown hair above his ear.

"All I know for sure is this, Gretchen. God cared about Maddy. He loved her. And Maddy wanted to love Him in return."

Yes, Maddy had always longed for God, tormented that she'd left the faith but too wise and too scared to go back. She could almost hear her sister's frequent worry. "What if Brother Gordon was right? What if we've lost our only chance at Heaven?"

Gretchen jabbed the straw up and down in her lemonade cup, rattling ice. The noise seemed out of place here among the quiet tombs. "Do you think my sister went to Heaven?"

"I don't know." Again he answered honestly and she

was grateful. "No one but Maddy and the Lord knows what transpired between them in those last hours of her life. But she *was* on her way back to the mission. Don't you think that means something?"

Sincerity oozed from the man like whipped cream between the layers of a sweet cake. She wanted to believe he was the "real deal" as Maddy had claimed. But she always came back to the same thing. Maddy was dead. Where was Ian Carpenter and Isaiah House when her sister needed them most?

"Why did she leave there in the first place?"

He drew in a deep breath and leaned forward, shoulders hunched. His gaze grew distant. "At some point in her counseling Maddy hit a wall. She was afraid to face something from her past."

Gretchen knew Maddy held secrets. She also suspected what some of them were. "Did she give you any indication?"

Ian shook his head. "More than once she talked about needing to find her higher purpose. And then she'd clam up."

Gretchen froze. Higher purpose? A vision of Brother Gordon's gentle face reared up before her, urging her and Maddy to do things in order to attain their higher purpose. In the end, the higher purpose had been Brother Gordon's bank account and his desire to control others.

The memory had no place at her sister's funeral. She stood. The movement, coupled with the heat and fatigue, made her wobble. Ian reached out to steady her, his strong hand oddly comforting. She slid away from his touch, not wanting her reporter's objectivity to be hindered by the fact that the preacher was an attractive man and outwardly kind. The inner Ian was the one she needed to know about.

What was his part in Maddy's death? Was he as innocent and kind as he seemed? Or did he make false promises and give false hope to the vulnerable? She'd once reported on a ministry that had tragically convinced a suicidal teen to stop taking his antidepressants and spend more time in prayer. The boy had shot himself.

Did Isaiah House also indulge in unethical and dangerous practices?

A headache pushed at the inside of her temples.

It wasn't that Gretchen disliked preachers or religious groups. Not at all. Some were excellent, but the public had a right to know. Her job was to find out what the general public couldn't, to force charities, especially religious groups, out into the open. To make them stop hiding behind the cross.

An idea for a new investigative series popped into her head. After the hurricane, she'd worked day and night for weeks investigating distributions to the relief effort, uncovering any number of discrepancies, misappropriations and downright theft of public monies. She wasn't too popular with the local authorities but a couple of her stories had been picked up by the networks, and since then the station allowed her free rein.

She was a watchdog, a guardian for the people. Her viewers depended on her to shoot square. To help them choose the best groups to support and those to avoid. Gretchen took this responsibility very seriously. She and her family had once been duped. She didn't want such a thing to happen to anyone else.

The hair rose on the back of her neck. Had it already happened to Maddy?

"Would you mind if I visited Isaiah House?"

Blue eyes blinked at her. "Everyone is welcome at Isaiah House."

"I meant in an official capacity." She watched him closely, eager to see if the suggestion rattled him. It didn't.

Serene as a blue sky, he said, "We're an open book."

Satisfaction curled through Gretchen's mind. If Ian Carpenter and his mission had anything to hide, she and everyone else in Louisiana would soon know.

Chapter Three

"Ian, I think you'd better come outside."

Ian looked up from his desk at the heavyset young woman standing in the door of his ground-floor office. Tabitha was one of the day counselors who worked with the female residents. He thought her name was appropriate since the Biblical Tabitha had also been a servant to those in need.

"What's up?"

"The newswoman's here again. Channel Eleven."

"Already?"

When Barracuda Barker said she was coming to the mission, Ian hadn't expected her quite so soon. The funeral was only yesterday.

He pushed up from the cluttered desk where he'd been praying about the runaway he'd taken in last night. After two hours of negotiation and countless calls to other agencies for social services Isaiah House couldn't provide, he'd gotten the girl and her parents to agree to one more try. He only hoped things worked out this time.

As he came around the desk, Tabitha glanced down at his feet. "Another new pair of shoes?"

Ian held out the pristine white runners for inspection. "Like 'em?"

"Cool. How many pairs does this make?"

That was a question Ian would rather not answer. He gave away his shoes to the needy on a regular basis, but every time he passed a shoe store he came home with a new pair. All his friends teased him about his one vice, but try as he would, he couldn't seem to stop buying shoes.

"Don't start about the shoes."

Tabitha laughed. As a licensed Christian counselor, she teased him more than anyone, claiming his shoe buying indicated some kind of psychological disorder. He laughed, too, but sometimes he wondered about the compulsion.

They crossed the dayroom together and headed for the door of the converted home. The room was quiet by Isaiah House standards. This time of day, some people were in Bible study groups. Others were in classes or at jobs secured with the help of Ian and his small staff. Nobody sat idle around here for long.

Ian stepped out on the Southern-style porch. Sure enough, the Channel Eleven News van was parked at the curb and the blond reporter hopped out, photographer in tow. As he walked toward the mission the photographer aimed his camera at Ian and started shooting.

Ian stifled a groan. He really didn't need this today with all he had to do. Hopefully, after a few questions, she'd be on her way. After all, yesterday after the funeral when they'd parted ways, he felt they'd made progress, at least to the point of mutual respect.

"Gretchen," he said cordially when she approached the porch.

Her loose-fitting white jacket swung open as she extended her hand. Beneath she wore a tank top the color of his mother's daffodils.

"Reverend."

Ian let the emphasis pass, studying her with an intensity she couldn't miss. Though carefully applied makeup covered the dark circles, nothing could erase the hollow expression in her eyes. She had no business working today.

"How are you?" And he meant it. How was she after yesterday?

Her face closed up. "I'm here on business, not to be counseled."

Ouch. Apparently, his thought that they'd come to some sort of mutual understanding yesterday had been way off base.

Gretchen not only didn't want to discuss the loss of her sister, she wanted to forget that she and Ian had ever talked. Even if he couldn't understand her reasoning, he could deal with her rejection. Preachers felt the cold shoulder all the time. The woman had been through a nightmare this week, and she needed time to grieve. For her own sake, he hoped she would give herself a break. Grief was a powerful emotion that took a toll sooner or later.

He held open the door and stood aside to let her enter the cool interior of the mission. As she passed, a gentle waft of lemon, like the magnolia in the courtyard, tickled his senses.

When the occupants of the dayroom saw the camera, most of them scattered like startled mice. The one or two who remained stared in open curiosity.

"I take it you're here on that official business you mentioned yesterday," he said.

Her pixie face turned upward. Yesterday's predicted sunburn tinged her tilted nose and the crest of her cheekbones. As he'd noticed the morning Maddy died, Gretchen was a small woman with fragile looks. But those looks were deceiving. Unlike her sister, Ian suspected the reporter's backbone was solid steel.

"Channel Eleven is running a new series on compassion ministries. We'd like to include a piece on Isaiah House."

"Hatchet job or fair story?" He didn't know why he'd asked that. He wasn't usually defensive about the mission, but something in her attitude today made him uneasy.

"Everything depends on your cooperation. The more open you are with us, the better we can represent you to the public." As she spoke, Gretchen's gaze raced around the room, missing nothing. Not that there was all that much to see. Couches and a table, a tiny reception area with a pay phone, a TV and a few plants potted and tended by Roger. "The one thing I can promise you is to be fair. My stories are honest portrayals from the inside of ministries. The public has a right to know what they're supporting."

"I can't argue that, but I'm not really prepared for anything extensive today. I'm pretty busy." He glanced at his watch. "Could we schedule another time?"

Her eyes narrowed in speculation. "Have something to hide, Reverend?"

He was gonna let that pass. For now.

"Nope." He slouched against the reception desk, sliding one hand in his pocket. Feeling the little fish key chain calmed the jitters that had invaded his stomach. "But I don't allow anything to jeopardize the recovery of my people, either. I'm sure you understand."

"*Your* people?" She emphasized the word as though it was loaded with insidious intent.

Ian liked to be cooperative, usually enjoyed sharing his vision for the mission with others, but he wasn't interested in playing word games with a reporter looking to catch him in a slip of the tongue to boost her TV ratings.

"Look, Miss Barker, I'm a straightforward kind of guy. If you have questions to ask, ask them." He smiled, hoping to soften her bulldog attitude with a little friendliness. "Why don't we have this conversation in my office? I could offer you an ice-cold orange soda."

He would have had better luck selling sand in Saudi Arabia. Gretchen didn't ease off.

"Here is better." She flipped open a small spiral notebook. "Let's get started. Tell me about the mission. What exactly do you do?"

"Easy question." He smiled again. Might as well be nice about it. As his mother often said, he'd catch more flies with honey than vinegar. And Gretchen Barker definitely needed some sweetening.

He pointed to the large framed poster on one wall and moved in that direction. Gretchen followed. "Isaiah 58 is our mission statement. The scripture tells it all."

The same words were engraved on a plaque outside each entrance.

The photojournalist focused in on the Bible verses and then turned the camera back to Ian. In T-shirt and baseball cap, Ian figured he didn't look much like a preacher. And that was okay by him, considering the people he ministered to. Teenagers were far more likely to talk to jeans and T-shirt than a suit and tie.

"Jesus commanded that we serve others. Isaiah House tries to do that. Mostly, our outreach is to runaways and street kids, but anyone who comes through that door gets all the help we can give them."

"Very commendable," she murmured in a voice that was less than impressed. Her sharp, intelligent eyes studied his face, and Ian got the sense that she wanted to find fault. What had he done to earn her animosity? Was it because of Maddy? Or did she dislike ministries in general?

He gave it another shot. "Kids on the street need a place to go, a safe haven where they can get help. That's what matters to us. Isaiah House is not three hots and a cot, as the street people call a regular shelter. We help lost people, particularly teens, find their way again."

"Interesting," she said, as she furiously scribbled notes. "Would you mind telling our viewers about your program? What do you do that makes you different from any other shelter?"

"Lots of things."

Eyes narrowed, she shot him that sharp look again. "Care to articulate?"

Ian wished he'd had time to prepare. Isaiah House wasn't a shelter, per se. It was so much more. But every time he tried to express his vision, he came off like a fanatic. And the last thing he needed was to sound like a nut on television.

The photographer had moved away to point the camera down a side hall. Roger limped in their direction, carrying a stack of towels. When he spotted the camera, he did an about-face, disappearing as fast as his hip could take him back toward the dining room. Ian couldn't hide the smile.

"I suppose our most important difference is this—we minister to the whole person, not only the physical. Humans are three parts—mind, spirit and body. If one is out of order, the rest suffer."

"Is there more emphasis on the spiritual aspect than the others?"

He paused to consider the motive behind the odd question, choosing his words carefully. "We use a balanced approach."

"Do you consider it balanced to require chapel twice a day, along with a Bible study and a prayer group?"

Okay. Now he saw where she was headed. Here was his opportunity to share his rationale, not only with her, but with a wide TV audience. "Yes. I do."

But before he could explain further, she interrupted him with another question.

"Can you discuss where the mission gets its operational funds?"

Money. Dismay filtered over him like a fog. To the press, ministries were about money, not helping people. The whole idea tore him up. No man in pursuit of wealth would choose to deal with the troubled castoffs of society. Why couldn't the public and the press understand that?

"We depend entirely upon donations."

"What about government funding?"

"No."

"Why not?"

"Because then we'd have to follow their rules, and we can't do that."

"Isaiah House has no rules?" She scribbled something else on her notepad.

"We have plenty. Biblical rules, not rules of the government."

"So let me make sure I have this right. Anyone who comes to Isaiah House for help is required to attend all the religious elements of the program. The Bible study, prayer groups and chapel. Is that correct?"

Ian had enough experience with opposition to know she was fishing for a negative angle, but all he could do was answer honestly and let God take care of the results.

"The only way to get people to change their lives is to change their hearts."

A smile, the first one he'd seen, softened the line of her mouth.

"Wasn't there a recent lawsuit filed against Isaiah House for expecting a man to attend a Bible study in exchange for a meal at the soup kitchen?"

No big news there. "Yes, but the courts refused to hear it."

"Were you guilty?"

"If you're asking if we require chapel or Bible classes to utilize our services, the answer is yes." His easy admission seemed to catch her off guard. Good. She'd been trying to catch him off guard from the get-go. "People can't change their hearts unless their minds are changed."

"You change their minds through Bible study? Isn't that brainwashing?"

Ian fought against rolling his eyes. Brainwashing. Please.

"The Bible teaches that we are transformed by a renewing of our minds. As a person replaces his old destructive thoughts with God's word, he's reprogrammed to think in productive, healthy ways."

Did that sound as stiff and religious as he feared?

"Reprogrammed. I see." She started to wander about the small room, gnawing on the end of her pen.

The chapel door swooshed open and a teenage girl stepped out, head down, a Kleenex clutched in one hand. Ian groaned inwardly. *Chrissy.* The one person in the mission who did not need to be confronted by a news camera.

Before he had a chance to stop her, Gretchen walked up to the girl and said, "I'm Gretchen Barker with Channel Eleven News. Could I have a word with you?"

Chrissy's eyes widened. She started trembling, her gaze darting desperately around the room in search of escape. They landed on Ian.

"Ian?" she croaked out.

Ian sprang into action, stepping between Chrissy and

the camera. Jaw hard enough to snap, he bit out one word. "No."

Gretchen stared up at him, clearly startled by the sudden change in his mild demeanor. "Why not?"

"Our residents have a right to privacy."

"Can't she speak for herself?"

"No."

For a matter of seconds, Ian and Gretchen stared, locked in a battle of wills. There were some things in this mission that no one, certainly not a news reporter, needed to know.

Behind him, the chapel door opened and closed. Ian relaxed a little. Chrissy had escaped back to the safety of the chapel out of range of the prying camera.

Gretchen was none too pleased at his interference. Eyes arcing green fire, she continued to stare at him for several long challenging seconds. Let her think what she would. Ian refused to budge.

Finally, she snapped her notebook shut. "All right then." She turned to her videographer and hitched her head toward the door. "I think we have plenty for this first time."

The shock of her words rattled Ian's brain.

First time? Did that mean she'd be back for more?

At seven o'clock Ian readied his notes for the evening chapel service. Tonight he'd speak on spiritual freedom, one of his favorite topics. Maybe the reminder would lift this heaviness from his spirit. He couldn't seem to shake the sense of failure over Maddy and the worry about her sister's sudden interest in Isaiah House. He'd done nothing illegal, but the news media could make or break a ministry. From Gretchen's attitude, he feared she wanted to do the latter.

He left his office and started through the dayroom to the chapel.

"Hey, Ian," one of the residents called. "You're on TV."

The Barracuda's report. The woman didn't let any grass grow under her feet. Though he'd thought of little else all afternoon, he hadn't expected the story to be aired this soon.

"You're famous, man," another called. "Can I have your autograph?"

"Do I look good?" he joked in return, coming to stand behind a long couch which faced the only television in the building. He leaned his legs against the slick vinyl fabric.

"That lady reporter must have thought so. She stuck around here long enough."

Accustomed to their good-natured teasing, Ian chuckled. "I don't think she was here because of my pretty face."

"Must have been the shoes."

Henry, whose shaved head was furrowed like a cornfield, said, "Yeah, that's it, man. The shoes."

"I think she was looking for me." Raoul was a street-savvy seventeen-year-old with a missing front tooth and a wicked sense of humor. "I sure do like blondes."

Ian thumped the teen on the shoulder. "She's too old for you."

"But not for you."

Henry's comment made him uncomfortable, though

he didn't know why. They were always ribbing him over his single status. Some day he hoped to find the right woman, but Gretchen Barker? Come on. Definitely not his type.

He frowned the teen into silence. "Be quiet so we can hear the story."

The knot in his shoulder started acting up again. Though he was praying against a hatchet job, he didn't have much hope.

The segment opened with the words of Isaiah 58 superimposed over a nice shot of the property. Gretchen's warm, modulated voice-over introduced the mission and Ian. As the story proceeded, the tension in Ian's shoulders slowly relaxed. Gretchen was doing a pretty decent job. The piece unfolded, straightforward, objective, clear, even if he did look more like a mission resident than the director.

Maybe some positive publicity would increase the lagging donations, and he could replace the ancient heating unit before next winter.

He came around the couch and sat down just as Gretchen said, "This reporter, in keeping with our commitment to truth, believes our viewers have a right to know that here in this lovely old house surrounded by the lush beauty of magnolias and wisteria, something sinister may be occurring."

A clip of yellow police tape from the scene of Maddy's death flashed across the screen.

Ian's heart thumped once, hard. He sat up straight and leaned forward. What was she doing?

The camera panned to Ian's face as Gretchen continued. "The boyishly handsome street preacher freely admits to using unorthodox methods and refusing government funds so that he can make his own rules. Rules that unfortunately include, by the reverend's own admission, mind control and brainwashing."

"I admitted no such thing," Ian sputtered, and then watched in horror as the camera showed him stepping, fierce-faced, in front of Chrissy. Thank goodness, the runaway's identity was blocked from view by his shoulders.

"Whoa, Ian," someone said, "you looked mad."

He hadn't been mad. He'd been concerned for Chrissy's safety, but Barracuda Barker hadn't recognized that reaction any more than Raoul had.

"As you can see from this video, we attempted to speak with one of the residents of Isaiah House, but Reverend Carpenter would not allow this. We plan to find out exactly why, so join us for our next segment of 'Behind the Cross' when we will delve more deeply into the secrets of Isaiah House Mission."

Ian sank slowly back against the cushions in stunned silence and put his face in his hands. He had a feeling his troubles with Gretchen Barker had only just begun.

Chapter Four

The familiar hustle and bustle of a busy newsroom flowed around Gretchen's cubicle. Phones rang, people talked in soft tones, a fax machine whirred. The mug of coffee on her desk grew cold. Head bent in total focus, Gretchen pounded the keys of her laptop, writing up the notes from her phone call to Marian Jacobs. Suspecting that some of the councilwoman's statements about Isaiah House were politically motivated, she would be very careful to research every complaint before taking them to the air. Keeping her integrity as an objective reporter was paramount, regardless of her personal concerns about Ian Carpenter and the rescue mission.

A creepy feeling, as if she was being watched, came over her. She glanced up.

The Isaiah House minister stood in the open space, one wide shoulder against the doorway, his hands steepled in front of him. Above gleaming new black-and-turquoise tennis shoes, faded old jeans and a turquoise T-shirt, he was rumpled and unshaven. A weathered LSU ball cap was pulled low over his face. The unexpected scruffy look gave Gretchen a sudden attack of butterflies. She had never met a preacher who looked so little like a minister and so much like a man.

Goodness. His eyes were blue.

"Got a minute?" he asked in that quietly compelling voice.

She took a second to casually toss an empty yogurt container into the trash can before pushing back from her desk. "Is this about last night's story?"

Even though she'd aired nothing but facts, Gretchen fully expected him to be unhappy with the report.

He sidestepped the question with one of his own. "Do you blame me and the mission for what happened to Maddy?"

The memory of her sister's untimely death, never far away, rushed in like a cruel wave of fresh pain. She closed her eyes, quickly collecting the loose ends of her composure before looking back at him. "Leave Maddy out of this."

Ian pushed off the flimsy partition and moved closer. Gretchen's pulse gave a funny jump of fear, but she couldn't quite pinpoint the reason. Was she afraid of him? Or of the odd reaction she was having to him this morning? Whichever, she refused to cower.

Her story had been fair. She'd reported what she'd witnessed, and from the way her e-mail inbox had overflowed, the people of New Orleans wanted to know more. Even if Ian was angry, what could he do in a crowded TV station? Laser her to death with his startling eyes?

He startled her even further by going to his haunches next to her chair so that they were eye level. The action stirred a vague scent of laundry soap and new shoes. For a second, she thought he was going to touch her, but when she stiffened, he placed his hand on the edge of her desk instead.

"It's okay to talk about Maddy," he said gently. "It's even okay to be angry about what happened. Shoot, *I'm* angry about it; you have to be."

His kindness was so unexpected that the horrible grief threatened once more to well up and flow out like a geyser. She needed to talk. She needed to make sense of her sister's life and death. And she needed someone or something to blame for the unspeakable waste.

With sheer force of will, she staunched the threatening tears. "Don't give me your counseling mumbo jumbo. I'm not one of your runaways."

He pinned her with a long, quiet look, holding her gaze until she fidgeted and glanced away.

"No harm or insult meant, Gretchen. Everybody hurts."

When she remained there, staring inanely at the slide show of monster trucks on her screen saver, the preacher pushed to his feet and stepped away. Gretchen breathed a sigh of relief. He was too close, both physically and emotionally, and she didn't want to lose control in front of a man she was investigating. What kind of objectivity would that be?

"So, exactly why did you come here this morning, Reverend? To complain about the report? Or what?"

He answered with a smile that probably melted everyone else. “I have a complaint and a suggestion. Your report wasn’t fair.”

“Viewers have a right to know the truth.”

“That’s all I’m asking. Report the whole truth, all of it. Show what we really do at Isaiah House.”

“Meaning?”

“Come to the mission. Spend more time with us.”

That was already in her plans. She propped an elbow on her desk and pointed at him. “On your terms? Or mine?”

“I was hoping we could make a deal.”

“Why, Reverend, you shock me. Making deals. Isn’t that rather unreligious?”

“I shock my mother sometimes, too, but she still loves me.”

There he went again, trying to use that sweet, Southern boy charm.

“You actually have a mother?” She bit the inside of her lip, wishing she hadn’t said that. The flippant remark sounded too conversational, too friendly.

“I have a great mother up in Baton Rouge. She makes the best gumbo north of New Orleans. When Dad was alive—” He stopped as if remembering this was not a normal chat between friends. Funny that both of them kept venturing into side conversations that had nothing to do with the topic at hand.

Gretchen tapped a fingernail on her desktop. Time to get down to business. Just because they’d talked at Maddy’s funeral didn’t mean she wanted to be buddies. “Okay, then. What’s your deal?”

"You come back to the mission. Not a one-shot deal like last time, but over a period of days whenever you have a free hour or two. No photographer. Volunteer, take part, follow me around. See what I do."

She couldn't believe her ears. A chance on the inside to see if his religion bordered on mind control? This was too good to be true.

"I've heard some negative rumors about the mission," she admitted. "I plan to check them out."

"I've heard them, too. That's why I want you to come see for yourself. All I'm asking is that you report the truth. I'll give you access. You give an unbiased report to the citizens of New Orleans about the work at Isaiah House."

This was too easy. What was he up to? She decided to test the waters and find out how much access he planned to give her. "What about your followers? Can I talk to them?"

Something flickered across his face that she couldn't interpret. Her antenna elevated to alert. Now she was getting somewhere. What was he hiding? Why was he so hesitant to let her talk to the people inside the mission?

"They are not *my* followers. As I told you before, they're vulnerable, and I won't allow anything to impede their healing. You can only talk to them on one condition."

"Being?" He'd gone ballistic when she'd confronted the trembling girl at the mission. She didn't want a repeat performance of that, but she *was* going to talk to that girl and find out why she was so afraid.

"You ask their permission and mine, in advance."

Interesting. Did he want to prep them first? Warn them of what not to say?

The demand sounded suspiciously like something Brother Gordon often did. She and Maddy had been taught all the correct answers to give about the commune. And all the specifics to avoid discussing with "outsiders."

Energy bubbled up inside. She was on to something here. If she played her cards right, she could have the investigative news series of the year *and* find out if anything had happened to her sister inside that mission.

Before she could voice her agreement a male head sporting a tiny gold earring poked inside her cubicle. "Hey, Gretchen."

The preppy speaker waved a pair of tickets in his hands. "Got 'em."

For a second she forgot all about her visitor. In excitement, she leaped from her chair and squealed, "I can't believe it. Let me see."

She ripped the tickets from his hand. David Metzler was not only a great coworker and friend, he was an absolute genius when it came to finding tickets to sold-out events. A computer engineer with enough brains to fill the Superdome, David was as passionate about Monster Trucks as she was.

She quickly perused the tickets, then threw her arms around his lanky form. "You are awesome! This is going to be so much fun. I've wanted to see Bigfoot and Grave Digger go head-to-head for two years!"

David's dimples flashed. "All righty then. See you tomorrow night. Six-thirtyish?"

"I'm there, buddy." They slapped a high five and David disappeared down the corridor toward the engineering room.

"Bigfoot?" Ian spoke from behind her. "As in monster trucks?"

In her excitement, she'd practically forgotten he was there. She turned toward him, unable to wipe the silly grin from her face. A night out, watching her favorite drivers and yelling with the crowd would work wonders for her right now. She couldn't wait to tell Carlotta that they finally had tickets.

She hitched a shoulder. "Everybody needs a hobby."

A half smile lifted the edge of Ian's mouth. "And yours is monster truck races?"

She slapped a hand on one hip.

"Got a problem with that, preacher man?" Goodness, that sounded flirty. She let her hand drop.

Ian laughed. The simple action did amazing things to his face. "You don't seem the type."

"Neither do you."

"All men like big, noisy trucks. Even preachers."

"I meant you don't seem the preacher type."

"Ah. Well. Thanks." He looked as if the statement pleased him. "I guess we're even then."

"Meaning?"

"Meaning stereotypes. Sometimes people judge you for not fitting the mold."

"I guess I did that to you, didn't I?"

"So, do we have a deal? You spend some time at the mission. Give us a chance to prove ourselves?" He flashed another of those killer grins. "Except for Friday night, of course. Can't let you miss Bigfoot."

Okay, so he was charming. And good-looking. Big deal. She was not about to get distracted by a gentle voice and a pair of gorgeous blue eyes. Not when they might hide a wicked heart.

As he motored down St. Charles Avenue, Ian dialed the Baton Rouge number on his cell phone and waited for the snick of connection. He'd been so busy he hadn't called Mom, something he tried to do every day. Since his father's death two years ago, he worried about her. At seventy-one, she was older than most of his friends' parents but refused to admit that age was in any way affecting her. She still gardened and ran the women's auxiliary at church, collected donations for the mission and swam daily at the health club.

A breathless voice answered the phone. "Hello?"

"Mom?"

"Hi, baby. How's my boy?"

Ian slowed to a stop, grinning at the traffic light above him. Even if he was approaching six feet tall and pushing thirty, he would always be Mom's "baby." An only child, she'd told him over and over how special he was because he'd come along after she and Dad had given up on ever having kids. His buddies had forever teased him about being a mama's boy. But he didn't care. He knew there was a difference between being a wimpy mama's boy and a man who respected and loved the woman who'd not only given him life, but a wonderful upbringing, as well.

Besides, the guys had all been crazy about her, too, and called her "Mama Margot."

"You sound out of breath. Are you okay?"

"Yes, of course I am." He could practically see her hand flapping away the suggestion of illness. "I was in the garage and I like to broke my neck getting to the phone. That silly dog is always underfoot."

That silly dog, as they both well knew, had become her best friend since Dad's passing. An odd mix of Irish setter and schnauzer, Nehemiah had been nothing but a ball of fluff abandoned in a box outside the high school football stadium. Ian rescued him and the grateful dog had never forgotten the favor.

"Give him a pat for me."

"Will do. He wishes you'd come for a visit."

Which meant Mom was missing him. Guilt twinged as he pulled away from the traffic light and motored along beside the St. Charles Streetcar. Filled with tourists this time of year, the old green trolley meandered along the edge of the beautiful Garden District, a neighborhood of wonderful old homes with verdant courtyards and ancient oaks. After the hurricane, he was glad to see the streetcar up and running again.

"I guess you haven't changed your mind about moving down here with me," he said. Mom loved this part of New Orleans.

"No, son, I haven't. Everything I know is here. My church, my friends, our house. I'm too old to start over."

Responsibility was a heavy thing. Ian adored his mother. He'd been so lucky to have great parents and he knew it. He'd been the center of their universe, but now that he lived in New Orleans he felt bad about leaving his mother alone in Baton Rouge. She'd always been there for him. He wished he could do the same for her.

Because they'd had this conversation a dozen times before, his mother said, "You have your own life, Ian.

You are right where God called you to be. I wouldn't have it any other way. Your daddy and I are so proud of what you do."

Mom still talked about Dad as though he was in the living room.

"I know, Mom. I know."

Her sweet encouragement made him feel even guiltier. He never wanted to disappoint her. "So, did you make that doctor's appointment like I asked?"

A momentary silence told Ian she hadn't.

"I'll try to get to it next week."

"Mom, you need a checkup."

Last week at the health club, she'd had a "spell" as she called the episode of dizziness and fainting. If the proprietor hadn't phoned him, Ian would never have known she was ill.

Mom, apparently, wasn't going to discuss the incident further. "George Bodine passed on Tuesday. Do you remember him? He used to give you gum in church."

Ian remembered. In fact, those were some of his earliest memories. He couldn't have been more than five or six when Mr. Bodine snuck Juicy Fruit to him over the pew. Mama couldn't figure out where he was getting the gum for the longest time. It was a huge joke between him and Mr. Bodine.

"I'm sorry to hear that. Should I send flowers?"

"Peggy would appreciate it. Or a card with a note about the gum incidents would be even better. She'd cherish the memory."

So did he. "Consider it done."

"The funeral was so nice," his mother went on. "Afterward the ladies' auxiliary fixed a wonderful dinner for all the family. Their daughter from San Antonio asked about you. You remember Sara."

At the mention of dinner, his belly growled. Refusing to take the bait about the still-single Sara, he glanced at the clock on the dash. Had he eaten at all today?

"Mom. You're avoiding my reason for the call. I insist you go for that checkup next week."

"Trying to make me feel old, aren't you?"

"You'll never be old." He pulled the van into the parking space behind the mission. If he hurried, he could grab a bite to eat before heading out on the streets for the night. "But everyone gets sick now and then."

"All that's wrong with me is a pair of empty arms. As soon as you get married and give me some grandchildren, I'll be right as rain."

He chuckled into the flip phone. "In God's time, Mom."

"You keep saying that, but I don't even think you're looking. You're so busy with those street kids—and I'm not complaining about that—but son, you need a social life, too. You need to get out more. Maybe even get an apartment away from Isaiah House."

"Can't afford it."

"I can."

"Not a chance." Dad had left her well-set, but Ian didn't depend on his parents' comfortable income. Not since graduating from college. In truth, he had a decent enough salary, but he plowed most of that money back into the mission.

"You have the assets Dad left. You've barely even touched them."

"Someday, Mom, when I get married and have a family. I'll need that money a lot more then than now."

She sighed heavily, her breath a gust through the cell phone. "Okay. I know when to hush."

"Call me when you make that doctor's appointment."

"Will do."

"Love ya, Mom."

"I love you, son. Come when you can." The phone clicked in his ear as she rang off.

Ian flipped the telephone closed and sat at the wheel of his van for several seconds. To his left, Raoul sweated as he pushed a mower over the grass where Maddy's body had been found. The gnawing in Ian's stomach turned to acid. Life was incredibly short and unpredictable. So many to help. So little time.

He had a meeting with the lawyers tomorrow, potential donors coming in the next day, his usual overload of counseling and Bible teaching, the street work with the homeless, the phone calls to arrange jobs and school and a ton of other details, and the worry about Gretchen Barker dogging his footsteps. He was tired to the bone, hungry as a wolf and sorely in need of some downtime to pray and study and sleep. But someday soon, he had to get up to Baton Rouge.

Chapter Five

"Ever volunteered in a soup line?"

Ian Carpenter lounged against the counter inside the large dining room of Isaiah House, a box of plastic gloves dangling from one hand. This was the first time he'd slowed down since Gretchen had arrived.

Taking his question as a challenge, she tied a snowy white apron behind her back and yanked the box from him.

"I can handle it." Any idiot could ladle soup.

One eyebrow twitched. "Just remember to be nice."

Did he truly think she would mistreat people because they were homeless? She shoved her hand into a glove, giving it an emphatic pop. "I'm always nice."

Ian laughed and moved off. She made a face at his back.

Fifteen minutes later, she understood his warning.

Some of these people stunk.

Gretchen fought a wave of nausea as she dished up yet another plate of beans and franks. Didn't anyone else notice the smell?

The girl next to her, one of Ian's runaways with a none-too-happy disposition, slapped a hefty slice of corn bread on the plate and handed it to an odorous woman.

Although she was a journalist and considered herself well-informed, Gretchen was shocked at the number of women, children and young people coming through the soup line. Weren't the homeless supposed to be old men with alcohol problems? A lot had changed since the hurricane.

Careful not to touch her hands to her face, she scratched her nose with the sleeve of her blouse. Inhaling deeply, she tried to hold the scent of her perfume as long as possible.

Not everyone stank, but a lot of them did. And the balmy fall humidity didn't help matters.

Methodically scooping beans, she looked around for the preacher. She planned to keep close tabs on her subject, a not-so-easy task. He was in constant motion, carrying large pots of food, busing tables, mopping up spills, sharing a word and that magnetic smile. None of the work seemed too menial. None of the patrons too dirty or unkempt for a pat on the back or shoulder hug. But Gretchen couldn't help wondering if the preacher was putting on a show for her sake. Or rather, the sake of her story. She'd need more than a couple of hours to make that kind of judgment.

At the moment, he was crouched in front of a little girl perhaps eight years old with kinky hair and big sad eyes. He reached into his pocket and handed the child something small, though Gretchen couldn't see what it was. The little girl smiled shyly and offered a hug. Gretchen's stomach lifted at the sight of the big, white man gently embracing the small, dark child as her pregnant mother stood smiling.

"Hey, lady, got any T-bone steaks back there for your best customer?"

Gretchen brought her attention back to the line of people. A grizzled old man who fit her preconceived image of the homeless grinned toothlessly in her direction.

"One T-bone coming up," she joked as she fished in the beans for a couple extra franks and plopped them onto his plate with a flourish.

"Now you're talking," he said. "You're new here, aren't you?"

"First time tonight." And already her best silver blouse was spattered with sauce, and she'd gladly change her snazzy heeled sandals for a pair of well-worn sneakers. No wonder Ian dressed so casually.

"You a volunteer or an inmate?"

The word inmate jumped out at her. "Volunteer."

"Glad to see a pretty new face back there. Preacher isn't much to look at."

She could argue that, and from the glances Ian was getting, so could a lot of other females. The preacher himself seemed oblivious.

The old man took his plate and said, "Name's James. Brother James Franklin Bastille."

He offered his free hand. Gretchen refused to be repelled by the stained and yellowed fingers. She whipped away the plastic glove and stuck her hand across the counter.

"Gretchen Barker. I'm happy to meet you, Brother James. You come here often?"

From the back of the line someone said, "Save the introductions for later. The rest of us are hungry, too."

Gretchen widened her eyes at Brother James and shrugged. He chuckled. "Come talk to me later. I got something to tell you."

Leaving her curious, he took his plate and shuffled off to find a table.

For the next hour Gretchen dipped and served and tried hard to remember, as Ian had said, that every person in the place was a human being with a story. The journalist in her found that fascinating. Her fastidious side was horrified.

When the line slowed, she made a point of going to the tables to talk to Brother James and a number of other "guests." They not only told stories of their own, they had stories about Ian Carpenter. A good reporter knew when to shut up and listen.

By the time the kitchen was closed for the evening, Gretchen's feet ached and her head swam with information. Even though she'd yet to hear anything too negative on Ian Carpenter, she couldn't wait to get to her laptop and type up her notes.

Untying her apron, she placed the now-dirty coverup in a bin marked for laundry. Wearily, she ran a forearm over her brow. After a day at the station, an evening here wore thin in a hurry.

Ian came round from the dining room, carrying a filled garbage bag. When he saw her, he stopped and hefted the bag over one shoulder like Santa Claus.

"Tired?"

"A little."

The corner of his mouth lifted. “So, what did you think?”

She shrugged. “Interesting.”

“That’s all you can say? Interesting?” He hefted the other two trash bags and moved to the back door.

Gretchen followed. “Actually, I mean it. Some of these people are fascinating.”

He, on the other hand, remained a virtual mystery. She’d come here to investigate *him* and so far, she’d learned little that she didn’t already know. But she had learned plenty about the myriad reasons for homelessness, information she could save for a future story.

Ian dropped the garbage bags out the back door into a Dumpster. His voice drifted back to her. “Interesting and hurting.”

Yes, she’d seen that, too. Even the ones who claimed to enjoy their carefree homeless life had come to the streets because of some pivotal, painful event.

Gretchen spotted yet another bag of trash and hurried to reach the back door before Ian could bolt it. Just as she approached, the lock snicked and Ian turned, slamming into her. She stumbled back, flailing for a handhold. Before she found purchase, surprisingly strong hands caught her upper arms and steadied her. His grip was sure and solid, a sign that this preacher did a lot more than preach.

“Whoa there. Can’t have a good volunteer falling into the kitchen sink.”

Blue eyes, both hypnotizing and serene, twinkled at her with an expression she couldn’t quite read.

They stood together, too close, watching each other

in the now too-empty kitchen. Ian smiled a mysterious half smile. Gretchen stared dumbly.

Somewhere in the building she heard voices and from overhead came the thump of feet. But in the dining area that had been so busy minutes before, she was alone with the troubling preacher. Not that this was a problem. She was an investigative journalist. Up close and personal with unsavory types was what she did. But unsavory wasn't the word that came to mind when she gazed at this particular man. And that was totally uncharacteristic for Gretchen Barker.

She was a newscaster, for goodness' sake, accustomed to thinking on her feet. Why couldn't she think of anything to say?

To her great relief, Ian broke the silence. "You did a good job tonight. I think you gained an admirer in Brother James."

His words were light, unaffected and about as impersonal as a letter addressed to "occupant."

Gretchen felt like an idiot.

To cover her discomfiture, she stepped back and forced a laugh.

"Brother James is a sweet old guy." Arms crossed, she rubbed at goose bumps that had appeared without permission. "He's smart, too," she babbled on, thankful to have found her voice. "Did you know he has a degree in literature?"

"No kidding?" Ian propped one hip on a kitchen counter and shoved his fingertips into frayed jean pockets.

Gretchen bit down on her molars, annoyed that he

somehow managed to be attractive in worn jeans and a baggy gray T-shirt stretched out at the neck.

Maybe he *was* using hypnosis on her.

She whipped around and began straightening the salt and pepper shakers. The little glass containers clinked together as she lined them up in neat rows.

"He graduated from Tulane," she said, determined not to be affected by his eyes or his looks or his soft words. "He was a professor there, too, until his wife died. Then his life fell apart and he took to the streets." She paused and turned around, an empty shaker in one hand. "He didn't admit it but I suspect he started drinking, too."

"He did. Spent half a lifetime lost in alcohol. About a year ago he found the Lord." Ian unwound himself and moved across the room in her direction. Opening a cabinet overhead, he removed a round carton of salt. Gretchen took it from him.

"If God fixed him why is he still coming here? Why hasn't the mission helped him get back on his feet?"

Ian spread his hands. "Some people are afraid of the real world, Gretchen. It hurt them before. If they go back, will it hurt them again?"

She unscrewed the lid and poured a steady stream of salt into the shaker. "But living on the streets without money or a home is much more dangerous!"

"Some don't see it that way." His gaze flickered to the doorway, and Gretchen had the distinct feeling that he was no longer paying a bit of attention to her. "Look, I hope you don't mind if I abandon you now. Some of the girls will be back in a minute to finish up here. I have to get going."

Just like that he walked out of the kitchen.

Gretchen stuck the salt back in the cabinet and banged the door shut. She quickly followed him into the dining area. "Going where?"

A beautiful young brunette she'd never seen before appeared from a side hallway. Gretchen's interest piqued. Either this was her kitchen help or the Reverend had a hot date. A very young hot date.

"Emily," Ian said. "Just in time."

The teen, tall and lovely enough to grace a magazine cover, smiled. "Chrissy and Michelle will be down in a minute. Chrissy's having another crisis."

Ian stopped halfway across the wide dining room and frowned. "Is she okay?"

"She wants to take off again. I told her if she left now she'd be sorry." The girl started to say more then glanced at Gretchen and changed her mind. Gretchen's investigative radar sprang into action. What was the big secret? And why would the girl be sorry if she left?

Before she could stop the comparison, Gretchen was thinking about Maddy. Had she been told that she'd "be sorry if she left"?

She hated being so suspicious, but painful personal experience had taught her to trust no ministry until she knew for sure it was on the up-and-up. Though Ian Carpenter appeared to be a good guy, he'd had complaints. And, frivolous though they seemed, there were those lawsuits.

"I'd better go talk to her." Ian started toward the exit leading into the hallway.

Emily shrugged and went to work, dragging a bucket and mop from the closet to fill with water and disinfectant. The scent of pine cleaner permeated the room in minutes. As casually as she could, Gretchen grabbed a wet cloth and began washing down the nearby tables.

"I'm Gretchen Barker," she offered.

The other woman glanced up briefly.

"Emily," was her only reply before bending her head toward the dirty wooden floor.

Gretchen waited until Ian's footsteps faded into silence. By now she'd worked her way to the table next to the brunette. "What's wrong with Chrissy?"

Emily slogged the mop into the water. "I'm not supposed to talk about it."

"Why not?"

She paused above the mop wringer. Her slender shoulders lifted. "Privacy, I guess."

"Who told you not to talk? Ian?"

"Everybody here. That's the way things are. If you want to live at Isaiah House, you keep your mouth shut about the other guests."

Gretchen wasn't sure how to read that comment. Either the mission protected its inhabitants or muzzled them.

"Guests?" she asked, liking the term far better than the word "family" that had bound her to the commune.

"Bunch of losers is more like it."

The young woman's vehement comment startled her. "You don't look like a loser to me."

In fact, Gretchen couldn't imagine why Emily was here. She didn't have that hollow-eyed druggie look that Maddy had. She was beautiful, well-dressed, intelligent. In fact, nothing seemed out of order.

The girl eyed her strangely. "If we're here, we're losers."

"I don't get it. Why would you say that?"

"Look. We all know who you are and why you're here, poking around the mission." She plunged the mop into the steaming water. Droplets splashed out, spattering the floor and further releasing the pungent scent of pine. "Ian's terrific. Leave him alone."

Emily's expression telegraphed a fierce warning. Hands off.

Hmm. Was there something personal going on between Ian and one of his very young "guests"?

Before Gretchen could dig further, footsteps sounded on the stairway and Ian breezed back into the room.

The angry look on Emily's face changed to a bright, model-beautiful smile aimed toward Ian. If he noticed, he didn't react. At least not in front of Gretchen.

"The others are on their way down," he said. "I gotta get moving."

As if Gretchen wasn't even in the room, he swung around and started to leave again. Wet cloth in hand, she followed.

"Where are you going?"

Ian didn't stop. "Street patrol."

Careful not to slip, Gretchen tossed the cloth onto a table and hurried after him, wishing for the hundredth time that she hadn't worn these snazzy little heels.

When she caught up to him outside the dining room, she asked, "What's street patrol?"

Three teenage girls clumped down the narrow wooden staircase, chattering in animated voices, and headed into the dining area. Gretchen recognized Chrissy from her last visit. The teen must have recognized her as well because she quickly averted her red-eyed gaze.

The need to talk to this particular girl stuck in Gretchen's craw. Sooner or later, she would find a way.

But right now, the preacher was digging in a hall closet and talking about something called street patrol. She had a feeling her night was about to get very interesting.

"What's street patrol?" she asked again, coming up beside him.

He pulled a backpack from the closet. The old house had dimly lit, narrow halls. Two was a crowd. She backed against the paneled wall, felt the cool smoothness through her blouse.

"Troubled kids hit the streets at night. So do I." He yanked a weathered ball cap from a shelf and shoved it onto his head, adjusting with both hands for a perfect fit.

"I don't get it. Exactly where are you going?"

As patient as the proverbial Job, he said, "I drive the streets, looking for runaways, kids who are too young to be out, kids in trouble. Or about to be."

He couldn't be serious. "Now? But it's after dark."

"That's the most dangerous time for the kids." He slid the backpack over one shoulder and maneuvered around her. The intriguing scent of soap and whatever made a man a man teased her as he passed.

"But when do you sleep?" she insisted.

"I usually get back in around one or two. I manage." He'd arrived at a side entrance by now. "This is what I do, Gretchen. If I'm going to minister to the runaways, I have to go where they are, when they are. They seldom come to us."

No wonder he'd looked frazzled and unshaven the other morning at the station. He'd been up all night.

"People have to sleep."

A wry grin lightened his face. "I can sleep when I'm dead."

"Well, you'll forgive me if I don't wait that long. What's the backpack for?"

"Essentials," was all he said.

"Wait a minute while I get my satchel," she said.

Ian froze with a hand on the doorknob. "For what?"

"To go with you. Remember? Total access? I'm your tagalong."

"I can't let you do that. You need to go home, get some rest." He stepped out into the black night and closed the door in her face.

Red-hot fury raced through her bloodstream. She yanked the door open and stormed out behind him.

If he thought he was leaving her here while he cruised the streets looking for teenagers, he was crazy. This kind of unorthodox concept of ministry was exactly what she'd come to investigate. If he didn't sleep, she didn't sleep.

Chapter Six

The night hung dark and sultry as Ian guided the rattling van through the cleaner, touristy area around Jackson Square and then into the seedier back streets of the ninety-block section known as the French Quarter. Neon lights pulsated over dark, mysterious entryways tucked into the long continuous brick wall of tiny shops, cafés, and bars. Zydeco music pumped out of a bar, stirring the air with frantic gaiety while Dixieland jazz thrummed from yet another. A flood of people, New Orleans's nightlife, roamed the streets or dappled the upper balconies of old historical houses turned business establishments.

Ian glanced at the woman in the passenger seat, wondering how she'd managed to talk him into this. He rarely took anyone with him, mostly because no one wanted to come along, but he also liked the freedom of doing things his way. He'd finally given in to Gretchen when it became clear she wouldn't back off. She was as much bulldog as barracuda.

He only hoped she didn't interfere. Or worse yet, scare the kids off. He had tentative, fragile relationships with any number of street people. All they needed to fade into the shadows was a strange face or the wrong word. He'd tried to explain this, only to have her promise to remain quiet. A newswoman remaining quiet? This he'd have to see.

"Where to first?" she asked. The flickering lights from the gas lamp flames glinted off her short, but very feminine blond hair and silvery blouse. As a rule, Ian tried not to notice women, certainly not their clothes or hair or how good they smelled. In his profession, as one of his friends had discovered shortly out of seminary, the wrong woman could ruin a ministry. But for some unfathomable reason, Ian was very aware of Gretchen Barker.

Maybe his mother had put ideas into his head, because after their conversation the other day Ian had started to feel lonely. Which was crazy. He was surrounded by people all the time, sometimes to the point of claustrophobia.

"There are some drug hangouts back in here." He made a left-hand turn, taking them deeper into the belly of the Quarter. "We'll check those first."

He didn't bother to tell her that he had a couple of specific kids in mind tonight. Kids that worried him because they were so close to the edge. Any day now they'd fall over into the cesspool of drugs, prostitution, crime.

"Crack houses? Oh, goodie." The sarcasm was not lost on Ian.

"Want me to take you home?" They rumbled past a row of bars, a voodoo shop, a sidewalk café.

She grinned at him. "You wish."

Yes, he did. And for more reasons than the news story. Tonight at the mission when she was unaware, he'd watched her serve up beans and franks. He'd watched her chatting with the guests as if they came from the upper crust. He'd watched her interact with the in-house kids at the mission. The barracuda attitude she took with him disappeared every time, replaced by kindness, even friendliness.

She was nice to others, but not him. Though he was working on the issue, one of his great failings was the need for approval—even from suspicious news reporters.

"So, who won the race?" he asked, remembering the tickets she's been so thrilled about the day he'd confronted her at the news station.

"Pardon me?"

"Bigfoot or Grave Digger?"

"Oh, the monster trucks." She twisted sideways in the seat to face him, her expression animated. "Neither, but the show was awesome. We had a great time. Have you ever been?"

Gaze scanning the sidewalks, he nodded. "The noise was deafening in a good kind of way." But not, as his dad had reminded him, any more deafening than the music he listened to.

"Yeah." She savored the word, grinning like a kid. "I love the noise."

"What about the guy at the station? Did he go, too?" He didn't know why he'd asked that.

"David? Oh, yes. He's a big truck fan." She laughed at the play on words. "I mean, he's an avid fan of big trucks...like me."

Another question was on Ian's tongue, but he drew the line at asking if David was her boyfriend. Her personal life was not his business. He wasn't even sure he liked the woman, and he knew she would skewer him on the six o'clock news at the drop of a hat. Thinking personal thoughts just showed how tired and overworked he was.

Although the curious question lingered, he clamped his mouth shut and drove in silence for a few blocks as he scoured the streets for a familiar face. If Gretchen noticed how quickly he'd ended the conversation, she said nothing.

They neared an intersection, and Gretchen pointed out the side window. "Look, the Tin Man."

At the apt description of the street performer, Ian smiled. On the corner, a man painted all in silver from head to toe had drawn a small crowd with his bizarre looks and accordion music. Beside him, a boy no more than eight tap-danced to the energetic rhythm while onlookers filled their box with change and dollar bills.

"Want to stop and listen for a while?"

She glanced at him, the green eyes catlike in the dimness. "I thought we were on the lookout for people in need."

"We are."

She thought about that for a minute before saying, "Do whatever you normally would do. I'm only the tagalong."

Ian edged the van to the curb. They couldn't stay long without a legal parking place and those were hard to find.

After he turned the key off the engine chugged for several more seconds.

"Sounds like your van is sick," Gretchen said as she shoved her shoulder against the sticking passenger door.

"Nah. She just didn't want to stop here." His humor was rewarded with a smile.

"Your van is a she?"

"Gotta be." He gave his head a sad shake. "She has a mind of her own, and she's way too complicated for a mere man to figure out."

This time Gretchen giggled.

A giggle? From Barracuda Barker? He didn't know she had it in her. And to tell the truth, he liked the fresh, feminine sound.

With that troubling notion rolling around in his head, Ian hopped out and rounded the vehicle. The Tin Man ripped into "When the Saints Go Marching In," the accordion pumping back and forth with amazing speed. The Tin Man always saluted his arrival in this manner, though Ian never knew if the music served as a greeting to him or a warning to the others.

As they neared the small gathering, Ian spotted familiar faces and stopped to say hello. He kept the conversation low-key and friendly. They knew who he was and what he stood for. Hammering the message home would only drive them away.

Though his mother would chastise him for rudeness, he didn't introduce Gretchen to anyone. A reporter in the midst would clear the streets faster than yelling fire. As it was, he was amazed no one recognized her.

She hovered at his elbow, thankfully saying nothing for the moment. He would hardly have known she was there except for her magnolia fragrance, a pleasant respite from the mingling smells of humanity, aged buildings and thick river air.

He kept an eye out for kids in general but especially for those who'd come to Isaiah House for help and had left without it. As always, his heart expanded with an odd mixture of love and pity for the street people.

"Hey, Preach." A boy with dreadlocks and a charming, open-faced smile sidled up beside him.

"Sticks," Ian said using the fourteen-year-old's street name. He had never seen the kid without a pair of drumsticks. "What's going on?"

Sticks loved to talk. The habit was useful to Ian, but one that could get the boy hurt out here on the streets.

Gretchen fidgeted at his elbow. He ignored her.

"Streets are pretty quiet tonight so far." Over the noise of zydeco music, Sticks moved closer to Ian and lowered his voice. "Posse got busted last night. Him and Spud robbed some old dude outside the casino."

"Did you tell his mama?" At sixteen Posse was out of control, but his mother sometimes rode the van with Ian looking for her son, asking Ian to pray. He always obliged, though he questioned the good either of them accomplished.

Sticks rolled a drumstick over one finger and under another. "Yeah. She's pretty torn up."

"I'll go see her."

"She'll ask you to get him out."

"I know." Hadn't he done that once before? "You

seen Terry Anne tonight?" The young runaway was heavy on his mind.

Sticks executed a silent drum roll in the air. "Saw her with some strange dude over on Frenchmen Street."

Some strange dude. Ian's heart sank. "When was that?"

"'Bout an hour, I guess. Might as well give up on her, man. Jackie ain't likely to let go now that he's got hold of her."

Ian fought the urge to agree. Jackie went through young girls like water through the swamps, leaving them soiled and broken. But Terry Anne had come to the mission a few times, and Ian couldn't give up hope that she could still escape.

"Thanks, Sticks. Anything else you can tell me before I head that way?"

"Check the alley behind Andre's place and the underpass down the street from there. Never know what you might see."

Ian nodded, understanding that this was all the boy could safely say. "Thanks. Wanna come back to Isaiah House with me?"

"Wasting your time, man. I'm hopeless." The boy laughed and tapped Ian with a drumstick. "Who's your lady?"

Ian didn't bother to correct the mistake. "Gretchen, meet Sticks."

"Nice to meet you, Sticks. A drummer, I guess?"

"Will be when I get me some drums." The boy guffawed, his dreadlocks wiggling like Medusa's snakes. "See ya at the Square next week, Preach?"

"Wouldn't miss it."

With that, Sticks moseyed on down the street, playing air drums as he went. In no way did Ian consider him hopeless.

"Interesting character," Gretchen said as they headed toward the van.

"Sticks is a good kid with a lot of potential. He just doesn't know it yet."

But Ian intended to keep on working and talking and building a relationship until he found a way to help the talented boy. Right now, environment weighed Sticks down. His dad was in prison, his mother dead. Sticks stayed here and there with relatives, but mostly on the streets. Even though Ian had invited him to live at Isaiah House more than once, so far Sticks had refused. As hard as that was for Ian to accept, there wasn't much he could do.

Gretchen broke into his thoughts. "Who's Terry Anne?"

The nagging worry returned. "A runaway. Really young and innocent. A sweet kid who should be back in Alabama cheering at football games, not hanging out with pushers and pimps." Though he didn't say as much, Terry Anne reminded him of Maddy.

"Is she underage?"

"Fifteen maybe."

"Why don't you report her to the police?"

"Some kids are worse off at home than on the streets. Besides, street people protect each other. No cop is going to find her if she doesn't want to be found. And if I turn her in, she'll not only disappear, I'll lose every ounce of credibility I have with the people out here. Then who will be there for them? Who will they have to call on when something happens? Right now, I've developed an uneasy acceptance from a lot of people who don't usually trust anyone. If I lose that, I'll lose them all."

He climbed behind the wheel and slammed the door, waiting to crank the engine until Gretchen buckled up.

"I guess I never looked at it that way," Gretchen said as they rumbled back onto the narrow street.

"Yeah, well, put that in your report. Street ministry is not clean or orderly or easy."

"Do you do this every night?"

"Mostly. At least for an hour or two. When I miss a night, something bad happens."

"Bad things happen anyway."

"True." But he always felt as if he should have been there. That he could have prevented trouble with his prayers and his presence.

There was a beat of silence before she asked, "Were you out the night Maddy died?"

He glanced her way, interested that she would mention her sister. The topic had been off-limits before.

"Yes," he answered. He'd been out but not long enough.

The van proceeded slowly down the narrow old streets past hotels and bars and vagrants. Gretchen sat against the passenger door, quiet and pensive. She had to be thinking of her sister walking these same streets, sleeping in the same alleys and doorways. Such thoughts couldn't be too comforting.

Ian's pulse accelerated when he spotted a young man in the doorway of a cheap hotel, cigarette smoke curling around his head. On the stoop next to him, a teenage girl was curled into a ball, backpack under her head, either asleep or passed out.

"Terry Anne," he said nodding toward the scene. "The runaway."

Gretchen drew in a hissing breath. "This doesn't look so good."

"You won't find anything good happening on this street." He wheeled to the curb and put the van in Park. As the vehicle went through the usual chugging and coughing, he said, "You'll probably want to stay here while I check things out."

Without awaiting her answer, he opened his door and got out slowly, assessing the situation as he moved. Behind him, he heard the metallic grind of the passenger door.

The tension in his shoulders tightened like a vice.

Just what he didn't need, and the very reason he'd wanted Gretchen to stay at the mission. A nosy reporter could get hurt out here. If not for his great worry that something very bad was going to happen to Terry Anne, he would turn around and leave right now.

"Jackie, how's it going?" Tone casual, he stepped up on the sidewalk, praying all the while.

"We don't need your help, Preacher."

Ian ignored the glower, focusing instead on the young girl, his heart heavy with the knowledge that she was probably high. Her skin was as pale as copy paper. "Is Terry Anne all right?"

"Yeah." Jackie laughed rudely. "She's had a busy evening."

Ian didn't even want to consider the meaning behind

that. "Why don't you let us take her to Isaiah House to sleep it off?"

The man barked another crude laugh and prodded the sleeping girl with the toe of his shoe. "Get up, sweet-cakes. Nap's over."

Ian gritted his teeth, his fists tight at his side, as the girl stumbled to her feet. Her hair stuck up in all directions. Beside him, Gretchen uttered a sound of protest and started forward. Ian put out an arm to stop her. She didn't know Jackie like he did. The man carried a knife in his boot and a gun in his pocket. This would require finesse, not force.

Gretchen apparently didn't agree. She refrained, but shot him a look of pure disgust. So she thought he was a coward. Nothing he could do about that.

"Terry Anne," Ian said quietly. "Are you all right?"

The girl blinked slow, uncertain. "Sure, Ian. Just great." She looked up at Jackie. "I'm great, aren't I, Jackie?"

Her girlish voice sounded frightened and unsure.

"You don't have to live this way," Ian said quietly. "We can get you help. Get you off the streets."

"I won't go back home."

"No one will make you do that, Terry Anne. I'm here to help."

Jackie flicked his cigarette onto the concrete and shouldered away from the wall.

"Look, Preacher, I told you. Terry Anne ain't going nowhere. Now get lost."

He shoved an open hand into Ian's chest, knocking him back several steps. Somehow Ian maintained his balance.

Fighting to keep a calm voice he said, "There's a better way, Jackie. Sooner or later, the streets are going to kill you. Both of you. You don't want that to happen. Neither do I. God loves you, man. He'll help you get out of this mess."

Jackie let out a string of expletives that burned the already heated air. Ian had heard worse, though he regretted Gretchen hearing the vitriol.

There wasn't much he could do but back off. "If you change your mind, you know where to find me."

"Yeah, yeah, I got your number. So don't let us keep you any longer."

He'd had this conversation with the pair for a week now to no avail. For some reason tonight he couldn't give up. His gut told him something bad was in the works. A small, still voice, the voice he was sure came from God, wouldn't let him back away.

"Terry Anne, you don't have to wait for Jackie. We'll take care of you."

The girl's eyes widened. She glanced from Ian to Jackie. The naked desperation in that gesture prodded Ian toward her.

With his peripheral vision on Jackie, he held out a hand to the girl. "Come on, Terry Anne. Come with us right now."

Jackie's tone threatened. "Back off, Preacher."

Ian's heart thundered in his chest. Keeping his voice steady and his eyes on the girl, Ian said, "Can't do it, Jackie. Not unless Terry Anne says so."

"Tell him, sweetcakes. Tell him to get lost."

The girl's lip trembled. Huge tears welled in makeup-smeared eyes. "But I'm sick, Jackie."

Ian took a step closer. He felt Gretchen move with him, felt her anxiety for the young girl. He kept his body between her and the unpredictable man.

"Just for tonight, Jackie? Please." A sheen of perspiration beaded Terry Anne's upper lip. "I think—"

At that moment, she leaned forward and retched violently. Gretchen rushed to her. Ian wheeled toward Jackie, daring him to interfere. Fortunately for them all, the man paled at the sound and sight of Terry Anne's sickness.

With a disgusted cry and another string of curses, he said, "Stupid girl's no good like that."

To Ian's relief, Jackie whipped around on gleaming black shoes and escaped into the lobby of the cheap hotel.

"Hurry before he changes his mind. He carries a gun."

Gretchen sucked in a startled breath and looked at him, green eyes round as headlights. Hadn't she even considered such a thing?

But to her credit, she helped the sick and quivering girl to the van, heedless that her own clothes were now soiled. Back at the mission and now here on the streets, Gretchen had done more than observe. She'd cared. And yet, she didn't like ministers and seemed intent on finding fault with Isaiah House.

He didn't understand her at all.

Gretchen Barker was a very puzzling woman.

Gretchen climbed into the back of the van, thankful to find a pillow and blanket waiting. Apparently, the reverend had done this sort of impromptu rescue before. As gently as possible, she helped Terry Anne get settled.

The girl trembled violently, sweat drenching her hair.

Gretchen prepared for another bout of sickness as visions of Maddy flashed through her head. She knew what to do. Hadn't she nursed her retching, shivering sister a dozen times?

The comparison ripped into her. Her own stomach churned, not with sickness but with grief.

Why had she thought she wanted to do this? To come out onto the streets with Ian? Hadn't she known there were others like Maddy still roaming the French Quarter in search of peace? Hadn't she realized that reminders would lurk on every corner? Hadn't she known this would hurt?

She smoothed a soothing hand over Terry Anne's forehead, aching for her lost sister. A pair of dazed brown eyes gazed up at her. In a heavy Southern accent, the girl murmured, "What if I get sick in your van?"

Ian twisted in the driver's seat. "Wouldn't be the first time. If it happens, it happens. No big deal. Try to relax and rest. We'll have you at Isaiah House in a few minutes."

He started the engine and pulled onto the streets, continuing to watch the hotel where Jackie had disappeared.

As soon as they were a block away, Terry Anne took a deep, shuddering breath and let her eyelids flutter closed.

"Are you okay back there, Gretchen?"

Gretchen's opinion of the street preacher rose a notch. In fact, tonight it had risen several notches. From what she'd observed thus far, his was a thankless job, and yet he persevered to the point of endangerment.

She glanced wryly at her filthy blouse and slacks. She stank and her snazzy sandals needed a wash. "Couldn't be better."

Ian caught her eyes in the rearview mirror and chuckled softly. "There are wet wipes and some other useful items in the backpack. Help yourself."

Gratefully, she found the wipes and used several on Terry Anne before attending to herself. The girl hardly stirred. Rings of exhaustion and illness darkened the delicate skin beneath her eyes. And she was frighteningly thin.

"This girl has been sick for a while, Ian."

"I was afraid of that."

"Is that why you pushed so hard for her to come with us?"

"Gut instinct. God wouldn't let me leave her there."

The phrase tweaked her attention. "Are you saying God talks to you?"

A blink of silence and then, "Is that a reporter question?"

Was it? Or was she asking because Ian was starting to get to her? Her stomach jittered at the thought. She'd been around people before who claimed to hear from God, and they'd used that power to control and manipulate. If Ian did the same, she needed to know.

"I'm here to do a story, Ian," she answered honestly.

"Then let's save this conversation for another time."

The evasive answer only roused her curiosity further. As an investigative newswoman, she probed into thoughts and beliefs to discover the real person hiding behind the public persona. Ian was smart enough to know that.

She squinted at his reflection in the rearview mirror. When they'd hit the streets, he'd turned his cap around backward like some college kid. Along with his usual jeans and tennis shoes, the casual look took years off and allowed him to blend in with the crowd. But now in dim shadow from passing cars and streetlights and framed by the outline of whiskers, his boyish face looked dark and serious.

Gretchen got the feeling that there were many layers of Ian Carpenter yet to be discovered.

"How do you keep your cool when somebody cusses at you the way Jackie did?"

"I wasn't all that cool. My natural reaction was to bust him in the mouth."

A preacher with violent tendencies? Or a natural male reaction? "But you didn't. Why not?"

"Well, the fact that he carries a nine millimeter in his coat and a knife in his shoe might have had something to do with it." His tone was self-mocking.

"That didn't stop you from pushing the issue when Terry Anne got sick."

"So I guess we're back to the same question, and I'm afraid the answer is also the same."

"God?"

"I sure couldn't do any of this on my own."

Once again she couldn't help comparing him to Brother Gordon who also claimed to hear from God. But Brother Gordon's mandates from Heaven had never put him in personal danger. Others maybe, but not himself.

And now here was Ian out on the dangerous streets confronting a man with a gun, a knife and a bad attitude because God told him to.

It didn't make sense. *He* didn't make sense.

It also didn't make sense that he had quietly slipped

money to several people tonight. Why had he done that? Was it payment for something? Or a gift of compassion?

Her head started to hurt.

She'd come to pry deeply into his life, but the closer she got the more of a mystery he became.

Yes, Ian Carpenter was a puzzling man.

Chapter Seven

"When can we expect something on this new series?"

Gretchen's producer, Mike Marsh, paced the length of the narrow meeting room. The hyperactive boss of Channel Eleven News never sat down during one of these production meetings, a habit that added to the stress of an already high-stress profession.

"I don't know yet," Gretchen said. "Three months for the full series. Maybe more. I was thinking an intermittent series might work best this time. The first ministry is taking longer than I expected."

After two weeks of digging, Gretchen was no closer to the truth about Isaiah House than before. At the mission, Ian seemed on the up-and-up. On the streets at night, he was a one-man wonder. But he still refused to let her talk to all the clients at the mission and now pressure from Councilwoman Jacobs, who somehow knew about the series, had intensified.

"Then move on to another and come back to that one."

"I'm doing research simultaneously, Mike." She held up five folders filled with contacts, pubic financial records, complaints, information from phone calls, e-mails and other sources. "All of these ministries deserve public scrutiny and they'll get it, but that kind of probe takes time. You want a thorough, unimpeachable series, don't you?"

"Without question, but—"

"Then give me the time I need to do this right. Don't I always come through?"

"How much time?"

She stiffened. "That's an unfair question, and I'm surprised that you'd even ask it. Investigative reports take as long as they take."

Mike ran a hand over his shiny, receding hairline. "We're not an independent news channel anymore, Gretchen. The big boys expect results for the money they pay out. We have to give them something."

"And they'll get it." A knot tightened in her belly. "Work with me, Mike. Tell the bosses I'm on to something big."

"Are you?"

"I could be."

He made a huffing noise and stopped pacing long enough to lean both hands on the table in front of her. "We seem to be having a communication problem today, Gretchen." His piercing stare seemed to look inside her. "Or maybe something else is going on here. Maybe Isaiah House has become your pet project. Is that the problem?"

"I don't know what you're talking about." But if he was thinking what she suspected, she didn't want to hear it.

Mike's expression softened a tiny bit, an unusual sight from the tough newsman. "Wasn't Isaiah House the mission where—"

She jumped in before he could mention Maddy's name. "I'm a professional. Personal feelings have no place in objective journalism."

Coffee breath inches from her face, Mike's intense scrutiny held steady. "My thoughts exactly."

Gretchen swallowed.

Even if his insinuation was true, she could still do her job and do it better than anyone else.

"You've had a rough few weeks," Mike said quietly. "If you need some more time off—"

"I don't! This has nothing to do with my sister." *Liar, liar, pants on fire.* The old playground rhyme danced in her head. She hoped the lie didn't show in her expression.

"The minister then? He's young, single."

That was enough to stiffen her spine. "I resent that implication."

A beat passed. The room was uncomfortably quiet. No one stirred, but Gretchen felt every eye watching her. Did they all think she was going overboard? Did they think she had a thing for Ian? Or a vendetta?

Mike broke the silence. "Then stop beating a dead horse, Gretchen. Unless you have something newsworthy, wrap up Isaiah House and move on. Today."

With a sinking feeling, Gretchen nodded. She grabbed her folders and ducked out of the meeting.

Was he right? Was she stuck on the little mission for more than professional reasons? She didn't want to think so, but Carlotta accused her of being fixated on Isaiah

House because of Maddy. David said she was getting fixated on Ian Carpenter.

They didn't understand.

She was fixated on the truth, whatever and wherever she found it.

An odd sort of confused discontentment shifted through her. She'd been searching for the truth all her adult life, and she still didn't have a clue what that was.

Gretchen heard a saxophone.

She quietly shut her car door and stared up at Isaiah House. Someone was playing the jazz saxophone as smoothly as a pro, only the melody was a very old spiritual.

Movement on the second-floor balcony caught her eye. Ian Carpenter, saxophone in hand waved at her. "Come on up. I'm practicing for a gig later on."

A gig? He played gigs?

She hurried up narrow wooden stairs that had become as familiar as her own apartment building. Ian's office resided on this floor, along with his private quarters. Not that she'd ever seen those.

Following the rich resonating melody through his office, she exited onto the balcony. When she stepped into view, Ian executed a rapid arpeggio, ending with a flourish and a cocky little grin.

"Hi."

"You're a musician." She slapped a hand onto her hip. "You didn't tell me that."

Breathless from the jaunt upstairs her tone sounded way too chummy. Not good. Not good at all.

Eyes twinkling, Ian trilled another fast run on the keys. “Quick. Call your news station with the shocking news. The preacher buys sheet music.”

In spite of her resolve to be tougher and get some final questions answered today, Gretchen grinned. Okay, so she liked the Isaiah House director. Good or bad, he looked great in T-shirt, jeans and backward ball cap, had a killer smile and played a mean saxophone. Better yet, he exuded nice. None of which would keep her from doing her job.

Even if she had to investigate on her own time, she planned to discover the real Ian Carpenter, whoever he was.

She plopped down in one of the metal lawn chairs. “I’m surprised I guess. You’re good.”

“You’re surprised I play or surprised I’m good?”

No false modesty. She liked that in a person. “Both. It doesn’t seem to be a minister sort of thing to do.”

He leaned the sax against a third chair and perched opposite her. He removed his Saints cap. Put it back on. His forehead puckered.

“Tell me something, Gretchen. Do you attend church?”

Whoa. Where had that come from? Her pulse kick-started. “No.”

“Did you ever?”

“Why are you asking?” If he was planning to recruit her, he was in for a big surprise. She would never be that stupid again.

“Because sometimes I wonder where you got this idea that preachers are not normal human beings.”

“That’s not what I think.”

Blue eyes probed as if they could see inside to the faith that had been shattered. "Isn't it?"

Memories rose inside, dark and bitter. She fought and failed to keep the anger out of her voice. "I know all too well how very human a minister can be."

All the more reason to ferret out the facts and motives behind every religious organization. Nobody should have to experience what she and Maddy had.

"What happened, Gretchen? What made you suspicious of religion? Who turned you off to God?" Ian leaned forward, face intense and earnest.

She was immediately suspicious. False concern was so typical of cultish groups. Yet nothing in Ian's manner seemed false. The conflict unsettled her.

Oh, what was she saying? Every minute around Ian was unsettling.

"Asking questions is my job," she said. Though right now she couldn't think of much beyond a churning need for personal resolution. Ian Carpenter was messing with her mind.

He steepled his fingers and bounced the thumb knuckles against his chin in the way she'd seen him do a dozen times. He really had that quiet prayer thing down to a fine art. That, and the gentle compassion that both comforted and annoyed all at once.

She feared he was messing with more than her mind.

"If you ever want to talk about it—"

"I've told you before," she snapped. "I'm not one of your runaways."

"Aren't you? Running from something, I mean?"

The soft question stabbed her in the heart, all the more painful because she thought he might be right.

"I had a bad experience. Let's leave it at that."

But he didn't. "With God or man?"

The question startled her. "I'm not one of those 'mad at God' people if that's what you mean."

"Then why did you stop going to church?"

She jumped up from the chair and walked to the balcony, her boss's words echoing in her ears. This conversation was getting too close for comfort.

"Look, Ian. I don't want to talk about my private convictions, okay? That's not why I'm here."

"But you want to talk about mine."

"Exactly." She refused to see the contradiction in that. She wanted a story, not a shoulder to whine on.

Behind her, Ian was silent. She could imagine him bouncing those thumb knuckles again in prayer. No one had prayed for her in a long time. Not real prayers for her benefit, anyway.

Below, a horse-drawn carriage clopped past, the chatter of the passengers rising on the wind. Gretchen let the silence on the balcony linger while she regrouped.

So far, all she'd unearthed about Ian or the mission were a few innuendoes, a handful of complaints and a bunch of unhappy neighbors. In the process, she'd started to like the preacher more than was sensible and to enjoy hanging out with him a little too much. But even though Ian *seemed* nice enough, she couldn't let go, she couldn't just walk away from the place where her sister had died.

If that was outside the realm of journalism, so be it.

She still couldn't shake the thought that something had gone wrong here before Maddy's death.

Hoping to catch Ian off guard, she sucked in a breath of hot, grass-scented air and whirled around. "Are you having an affair with one of the girls?"

Metal rattled against the wooden deck as he sat straight up, frowning in shock. "I can't believe you asked me that."

She couldn't believe it, either, any more than she believed him guilty of an affair, but that was one angle she hadn't pursued.

"Are you?"

"Of course not."

"Then why can't I talk to Chrissy?"

"I've promised to protect her privacy."

"For her sake or yours?"

His head dropped back. He stared up at the giant oak leaves hanging above them. The faint darkness where his beard grew outlined his jaw. She couldn't look away from the masculine image.

"You've been following me around for days. Have you found anything to indicate this ministry is less than honorable?"

"I've heard complaints." Allegations, gripes and innuendoes, but nothing hard and fast.

"So have I. The food's lousy. Water pressure in the showers is lousy. This morning one of the boys said I was too strict and he would rather live in a trash can."

"What did you do to him?"

"Something vile and disgusting," he said, the glitter of humor back. "I assigned him to clean toilets."

She wrinkled her nose. "You *are* cruel."

But a kid's complaint about toilet duty wouldn't get her a spot on the ten o'clock news.

"We all pull our weight around here. Including a turn at the toilets. The mission can't function unless everyone pitches in."

"What? No room service?"

His short bark of laughter said he appreciated the joke.

"No service at all," he said. "Just hard honest work and good wholesome living."

Honest. Wholesome. Good. Three words that seemed to fit Ian to a tee.

Her heart thumped once, hard.

It was definitely time for her to move on.

But she didn't want to. And she was terrified that her reluctance to pull off the story had little to do with her job, or even with Maddy, and a lot to do with Ian Carpenter.

She glanced up as he crossed one foot atop his knee. The bottom of his handsome pair of joggers was unsoiled. Another sparkling new pair of shoes.

Gretchen frowned.

Lots of women had shoe obsessions, but a man? And a preacher at that? "Is that another new pair of shoes?"

He grimaced. "Guilty."

And he really did seem to feel guilty about the purchase. She narrowed her eyes. Interesting.

"What was wrong with the other pair?"

"Nothing."

"I don't think I've ever seen you wear the same shoes twice."

Great. Now she was angling for a story on his shoes.

Boy, was she straining. As Mike said, she had to stop beating the dead horse.

He plopped the foot down onto the wooden terrace. "Is this TV report going to be about my footwear?"

She laughed. "Only if you spend all the ministry's money at shoe stores."

"I don't. I spend my own." He pumped his eyebrows. "Wanna go shoe shopping with me? My treat. I know all the best places."

"Well," she said, pretending to think. "I've always wanted a pair of Prada shoes."

Eyes round, Ian whistled. "I couldn't interest you in something slightly less…"

"Expensive?"

He tapped his lip once, then pointed at her. "That's the word."

"I don't know where I'd wear Prada shoes anyway."

"So it's a deal? You and me. The Riverwalk. If we go early, I'll even spring for coffee and beignets."

"You're serious, aren't you? You'd actually take me shoe shopping?"

"Sure. Why not?"

"Guys hate shopping."

"Tsk, tsk. Stereotypes. Blowing them out of the water is so much fun."

"You *are* good at that. But seriously, Ian, where do you get that kind of money? I've seen the mission's books." Roger had gone over the finances with her and answered her questions, albeit a little too carefully for her tastes but still he'd answered them.

"You don't accept much of a salary from your

board of directors. How do you afford to hand out twenty-dollar bills on the street and buy hundred-dollar shoes?"

If he was surprised that she knew about the handouts, he didn't show it. "I'm not into anything illegal, if that's what you're implying."

The idea had crossed her mind, though she'd found nothing to substantiate it. Still, a mission set up to help teenagers was the perfect cover for an illicit drug operation. Money had to come from somewhere.

"No implication, just questions." She kept her tone light, teasing. "After all, you're buying my next pair of espadrilles. I have to be sure I'm not taking funds from the hungry."

He tilted back in the chair, folding tanned arms across a white novelty T-shirt. "Your conscience is safe. When my Dad died, he left me some money. If I'm careful, I can get by on the interest. It drives my mother crazy."

"Why?"

"Because I'm her only child, her baby boy." He smiled at the admission, and Gretchen could well imagine his mother and any other woman succumbing to those blue eyes and sweet smile. "She wants me to have everything."

"Did you have everything growing up?"

"Everything I needed, I guess, and lots of extras. Life was good." His athletic shoulders lifted. "Still is."

Gretchen envied the way he said that. He saw the deepest despair of humanity and could still think life was good. She'd long since lost that naiveté.

"Your mother lives in Baton Rouge, right?" Gretchen wondered what a chat with the mother might turn up.

"Yeah. I want her to move down here with me, but she won't. She's too busy. I think the entire city would close up if she left town." Pride and love lit his face. "Mom's in her seventies, but says she has to stay in Baton Rouge to take care of the old people."

Gretchen allowed a smile. "Sounds like a great lady. Is she the one who got you started playing the sax?"

"I wish I could say yes, but that would be a lie." He shifted in his chair and gave a self-conscious laugh. "I learned to play for a shallow, totally male reason."

"To impress some girl?" she guessed.

He grimaced. "Please don't put that in your story."

She laughed. "Your secret is safe with me."

But she *was* curious about the kind of girl who could interest Ian that much.

"Was she impressed?"

"'Fraid not. She went for the drummer instead."

"Fickle females."

"My exact response. Lost the girl. Got the saxophone. A good trade if you ask me."

"It's a beautiful horn. I've never seen one quite like it."

He hoisted the sax, handling the gleaming brass instrument with obvious affection. "A vintage Selmer. Dad bought it for me. I never dreamed he'd spend that kind of money."

"Special occasion?"

His face took on a wistful look. "My sixteenth birthday."

"Most boys that age would ask for a car."

Ian's eyes twinkled. "He *wouldn't* have bought that. Dad was old-school. He said, 'If you're responsible enough to drive a car, you're responsible enough to hold a job and pay for it.'"

"Did you?"

"You've seen what I drive. What do you think?"

Gretchen giggled. His sense of humor got to her. "I'm sure that old van is not the only vehicle you've ever had."

No doubt, a good-looking guy with his charisma had driven the hottest car on campus and dated the prettiest girls.

"You think?" He arched an eyebrow and raised the saxophone to his lips. "What's your pleasure, ma'am?"

You.

The thought came out of nowhere, startling and unwanted. Her heart leaped. She fought down a telling blush and rising panic.

"Something sweet and lazy," she managed to say. Any distraction to help me get my head under control.

Ian pressed the mouthpiece to his lips and began to play. Thank goodness he couldn't read minds. She was having some serious trouble with hers at the moment.

Her gaze strayed to his mouth, pursed against the saxophone. What would it be like to have those lips pressed against hers?

She slammed her eyelids shut and leaned back in the chair. This nonsense needed to stop here and now.

The flowers from the courtyard were in full bloom. The scent of honeysuckle drifted up to the balcony.

Music vibrated on the air, gentle and tender as first love.

She was single. So was he.

Her stomach flip-flopped. There she went again. Oh, boy.

This sudden obsession with Ian as a man was all Mike's fault. He never should have asked her if she was interested in the preacher instead of the series.

Annoyed and flustered, Gretchen pushed out of her chair and went to the balcony's wrought-iron railing.

The music stopped.

"Don't like my choice of songs?" Ian asked.

She didn't care if he played "The ABC Song." She had to get out of here. She had to stop thinking of this preacher as an attractive man when he was supposed to be the subject of a serious investigative report.

Gripping the cool metal railing, she gazed out over the grounds, moist and green from the October rains.

"I know this will break your heart," she said a little too jovially, "but I'm wrapping things up here today."

A beat of silence told her he was surprised. "The report?"

"Yes." And the idea of leaving unfinished business didn't sit well.

"Tired of our company?"

Was that relief or disappointment she heard?

"You've become boring, I'm afraid." At least to her boss and the viewing public both of whom were primarily only interested in trouble.

"In other words, you can't find any reason to blast us on the news?"

She turned to face him and then wished she hadn't.

Looking too handsome for words, Ian was watching her, expression thoughtful. Her heart did a ridiculous, disturbing somersault.

"Just because I pull off for now doesn't mean I'm finished. I'm still digging for the truth."

A gentle smile tilted the corners of his mouth.

"The truth is right here in plain sight, Gretchen. All you have to do is open your eyes."

Now what on earth did that mean?

A vague sense of loneliness shifted through Ian as he climbed into the van for his Saturday-night street patrol. The fact of the matter was he'd grown accustomed to Gretchen's company on these runs. At first, when she'd told him the investigation was over, he'd been relieved. Surprised, sure, but also happy to be released from the pressure of a television newswoman watching his every move. He had enough hassle in his life.

But after a week without her around, he missed her. Not the bulldog reporter with the attitude, but the other Gretchen. The woman who could be witty and compassionate.

Besides, she liked his music.

Man, did he need a vacation or what? Nobody missed the Channel Eleven barracuda. Especially because of a high school vanity thing like music.

With a self-deprecating laugh, he tossed the refilled backpack into the backseat, ready for the long night ahead.

As he reached for his seat belt, a human form appeared around the side of the building. He squinted into the shadowy darkness. Was one of the kids out after curfew?

Better go check. More than one runaway had run away.

Releasing the belt, he shoved the door open. Into the

circle of light from the van's interior stepped the barracuda herself.

Ian's stomach went south in the most peculiar way.

She stopped not two feet from him, a hand on her hip. "Going somewhere without me?"

"I thought you were finished with Isaiah House."

"Officially, I am. At least for now."

"Then why are you here? Hoping to catch me in some ghastly indiscretion?"

A tiny smile tipped the corners of her shapely mouth. "Maybe."

Strangely disappointed by her answer, Ian turned back to the vehicle. Gretchen was getting under his skin in more ways than one. "Go home and sleep. You have a day job."

"So do you." She grabbed the door before he could close it.

He paused, wishing she'd leave, wanting her to stay.

Yep, he was seriously messed up. Slowly, he rotated toward her. "I gotta go, okay?"

Her big green eyes held his as firmly as her hand held the van door. "I'm here as a volunteer. You need me."

Yes, like he needed another pair of shoes. But something in her posture wouldn't let him slam the door and drive off. Framed by the glow of the dome light the confident newswoman looked small and uncertain.

Suddenly, he got it. Gretchen was the needy one. Perhaps she always had been.

"Maddy?" he asked softly, gently broaching the once-taboo topic.

"I need to help, Ian." A soft, sweet-scented breeze

lifted the ends of her pale hair. She pushed at it, self-conscious. "If we can save one kid…"

Ian smiled, understanding all that she couldn't or wouldn't say. "Contagious, isn't it?"

Her unspoken desire to make amends for Maddy's death resonated within him. Didn't he want the same thing?

To lighten the mood he said, "You have to buy the pizza."

Her shoulders relaxed. She patted her jeans pocket. "I got paid today."

"That makes exactly one of us." With a laugh, he motioned to the passenger's seat, suddenly looking forward to the long hours ahead. "Get in. Time to rock and roll."

Chapter Eight

As the weeks flew by and the holiday season approached, Ian grew comfortable with his Saturday-night running mate. The rest of the week she might be off harassing other ministries, but on their weekly jaunts she said little about her series. He wasn't naive enough to think she wasn't watching him like a hawk, but she was now more subtle.

Sometimes, like the afternoon they'd gone shoe shopping and he'd bought her a pair of sparkly heels for an upcoming office party, he even forgot her original reason for hanging around Isaiah House.

He knew she was still hurting over her sister's death. She was also suffering from some deep spiritual wound. Though she listened to him share Christ on the streets and stood quietly respectful when he prayed, she wasn't ready to discuss her own faith, or lack thereof.

Funny how that bothered him.

He glanced her way, throat tight with wanting to help her heal and not knowing how to go about it.

She was a tough cookie, he'd give her that. But underneath the strong exterior was a caring woman. He'd seen proof of that a dozen times over.

One dismal night beneath an overpass often used as shelter or for drug deals they'd found a dead body.

Gretchen reported an exclusive on that one. Though sadly, a dead homeless man didn't garner much more than a mention on the late, late news. No name, no humanity, just a dead body found under the freeway along with the instrument of his demise, a dirty syringe. And that was the way she'd reported the death, a stark, painful reality of life to jar the comfortable into action.

Tonight, they'd already unloaded a dozen sandwiches, dropped a homeless woman and her child at an appropriate shelter and counseled two teenagers with nothing but time and trouble on their hands. Armed with Ian's network of social and medical services, they could meet a lot of needs. At least enough that he could sleep without the nightmare.

"Are we cruising the bars later?" Gretchen's modulated voice was thoughtful as Ian parked the van along a dark side street.

"Maybe." When the streets were quiet, they often dropped in on the rowdier, seedier bars and late-night hangouts. He never knew where he might find a troubled kid or for that matter, someone looking for a listening ear or a prayer. At first, he'd been reluctant to take Gretchen inside, but true to form, she went anyway.

They walked quickly, both constantly alert to their

surroundings. Although the Café Du Monde was a popular tourist spot, the surrounding area was just as popular with the city's underworld. Runaways congregated among the panhandlers and homeless. Prostitutes and predators lurked here, as well.

"Hey. Hey." A female voice called. Ian turned around. "You really a preacher?"

A provocatively dressed woman sauntered toward them, a beer in one hand.

"Yes, ma'am. What do you need?"

She shifted her beer to the opposite hand and reached out for his. Her damp skin was hard and cool.

"I want you to do something. Something kinda weird."

Hair rose on the back of his neck. Great. He was about to be solicited, probably along with Gretchen who moved in close to his side. In an odd way her reaction made him happy. Gretchen trusted him to protect her. He trusted God for the same thing.

Gently holding the street-hardened hand, he purposely made eye contact with the obvious prostitute. Regardless of her lifestyle, she mattered. He wanted her to know that.

"Weird in what way?"

The woman's nose twitched. "I want you to pray for me."

Thank you, Lord. He'd been propositioned before but not with Gretchen along. "That's not weird at all. What's your name?"

Eyes really were the windows to the soul and hers were sad and empty.

"Leslie."

"Well, Leslie, I'm Ian and this is Gretchen. I'd consider it a privilege to pray for you."

He bowed his head, and on the dirty sidewalk beneath a pool of streetlight, he prayed for protection and comfort and healing in Jesus's name.

When he finished, Leslie's hard, damp hand hung on a little longer like the poor swimmer at summer camp who finds the rope in the middle of the pool and is afraid to let go.

It broke Ian's heart. "Can we take you somewhere, Leslie? To a shelter, maybe? How can we help?"

She held on a moment longer, then shook her head. "Can't. Thanks for the prayer."

And then she whirled and quickly walked away.

Gretchen touched him on the shoulder. Tears swam in her big green eyes.

Ian swallowed a lump of sadness. If he did this for a million years, he'd never get used to the despair. He could offer all the help in the world, but until a person was ready to accept it, both he and God were helpless.

Thanksgiving came and went. Gretchen worked at the news station. Ian served turkey and dressing in the soup kitchen and had a quiet dinner with his mother that night. Though she denied any further health problems, Ian's mother didn't seem her usual vivacious self.

Overall, Ian was feeling better about the fate of the mission. People were generous with charities around the holidays so donations were up and pressure was down. Though the lawsuit had cost them more money than was prudent, the plaintiff had finally dropped the charges when he realized Ian would not agree to a monetary settlement. Though he figured the question would arise again in the future, for now anyone using mission services could still be compelled to attend chapel. Except for Marian Jacobs, who, along with several local restaurants, had complained loudly about the stream of homeless at the mission on Thanksgiving Day, Ian had hope that things were on the upswing. The holidays always gave him hope, especially Christmas.

Early in December, he took the handful of Isaiah House residents Christmas shopping. Later, they transformed the old mission house with lights and wreaths and shiny garland. Generous donors made certain the kids had gifts beneath the artificial tree in the dayroom, even the ones who would go elsewhere until the New Year.

But when Christmas Day rolled around, Ian was on edge, for more reasons than one.

A couple of night's ago when he'd been too tired to think straight, he had invited Gretchen to Christmas dinner at his mother's house in Baton Rouge. Now he questioned the wisdom of such an action. Upon hearing that she planned to spend the day alone he'd issued an invitation out of courtesy. At least, he'd told himself that was the reason. Judging by the time he'd spent thinking about her lately, he worried that more than good manners were at play here.

Then this morning as soon as his feet hit the floor, two of the boys got in a fistfight over a pair of socks.

And now this.

"Are you sure, Roger?" A bag of petty cash was missing.

The older man's perpetually worried face sagged. "One of the kids must have taken the money out of my desk."

"When?"

"Don't know for sure."

"I can't believe it. In three years of this ministry, nothing has ever been stolen."

"There's always a first. You're a pretty trusting fella."

Maybe too trusting, but one of the things these kids needed most was to have someone believe in them.

The knot in his shoulder returned. He resisted the urge to rub at it. "If they needed money, they should have told me."

"Well, nothing to do about it today. It's Christmas. You go on up to your mama's. We'll question the kids when everyone gets back after the holidays."

As much as it bothered him to leave the issue unresolved, he'd have to wait.

"Sure you don't want to come along? Mama won't mind." He offered for the third time this morning.

"Thanks anyway, but I got plans. You and your mama can have a little one-on-one time."

"I invited Gretchen."

Roger took a second to absorb this turn of events and then cuffed Ian on the arm. "Taking her home to Mama, are you? About time a lady caught your eye."

Ian held up a five-fingered stop sign. "Don't go there, friend. You know how I feel about that subject."

His friend made a face. "Right. You're waiting for a wife to drop straight from Heaven."

"A Christian wife, Roger. That's the operative phrase. Gretchen knows a lot about religion, but she doesn't know a thing about a relationship with a loving God."

Regardless of the hours they'd spent together, Gretchen remained very cool to the topic of faith.

Some minister he was.

"I've never seen you spend this much time with a woman. You must like her a lot."

"She's doing a news story on us."

Roger's guffaw rang out. "Since when?"

What Roger said was true. Other than a nice piece about the annual Thanksgiving meal, Gretchen's series hadn't mentioned Isaiah House in a long time.

"We've been keeping a low profile, I guess. Nothing to report."

"All the more reason not to mention the petty cash problem. Gretchen would be on that like a duck on a June bug."

Before either of them could say more, a female voice spoke. "Are you guys talking about me?"

Both men spun toward the open office door. Ian's heart thumped once, hard, against his rib cage.

"Gretchen." He grappled for words, hoping she hadn't overheard their conversation. Neither the missing money nor Roger's suggestion that Ian was taking Gretchen home to Mama were topics he wanted to share with her. "You're looking good."

Real good. Her flippy hair was blonder, her eyes greener above a skirt and sweater the color of honeydew melon. Silver snowflake earrings dangled from her ears.

"Well, thank you very much." One hand holding her

gauzy skirt out to the side, she executed a quick curtsy. The action stirred her perfume and drew attention to her legs. Ian had a hard time not staring.

"Ready to go?" he asked. "I told Mom we'd be there by two and I need to run by the hospital first."

The topic of last night's trouble proved ample diversion. Gretchen had been with him. She knew what went down, and she'd been so shaken by the unresponsive, overdosed boy, she'd cried afterward. Her tears had really gotten to him.

"Do you think he'll survive?" Gretchen asked after they bid farewell to Roger and started down the steps.

"I hope so." He'd spent an hour on his knees in the chapel asking God to spare the kid and give him one more chance to help. "All we can do at this point is pray."

As they crossed the lawn Ian avoided the area where Maddy had died. The action had become such a habit he barely thought about it anymore, but Gretchen glanced quickly in that direction and then away.

"God doesn't hear my prayers, Ian."

A place inside him went still. "What makes you say that?"

"Experience." She moved a tiny silver purse from one hand to the other. "And no, I don't want to talk about it today either."

But she would. Eventually, he'd find out what had hurt her. He had to.

As soon as the van rattled into the driveway lined with Christmas lights, Mom flew out the front door of the comfortable suburban home where Ian had spent his childhood. Face wreathed in a smile, a red Santa dish towel over one shoulder, she threw her arms around her son. With a joyful laugh, he lifted her several inches off the ground, breathing in the welcome scents of Estée Lauder perfume and home cooking.

"Do I smell pecan pie?"

"What do you think?"

"I think I have the best mom in Louisiana."

This was their normal mother-and-son banter but this time Mom grew uncharacteristically serious. She whapped him softly on the chest with her dish towel. "Don't you forget that, either, young man. Ever."

Before he could read too much into the statement, she turned her attention to Gretchen and the moment passed.

"Oh, honey, it is such a pleasure to meet you."

With her usual Southern warmth, she reached out and grasped both of Gretchen's hands, eyes sparkling in a way that made Ian want to groan. He'd told her on the phone that Gretchen was a business friend spending the holiday alone, but his mother was a hopeless romantic.

"That TV report you did on Ian's mission at Thanksgiving was lovely."

As his mother led the way up the front steps, Ian and Gretchen exchanged wry looks, both aware that most of her reports about Isaiah House had been anything but lovely.

Once inside the fragrant house, his mother disappeared into the kitchen to check the hot rolls. Gretchen began to walk around the living room, looking at the Christmas decorations, the family pictures and keepsakes. Even with Mom's lighted village and other Christmas decor, no one could escape the room's main focus.

Gretchen raised an eyebrow at him. "The Ian shrine?"

He shook his head, embarrassed. "The curse of the only child."

Mom still displayed the tennis trophy he'd won in middle school; every degree, certificate and award he'd ever earned; band ribbons; and even a plaster of paris handprint bearing his name and the date. He'd made the thing in Bible School when he was in second grade.

Gretchen trailed a finger over a childishly crafted felt ornament. His teeth, too big for his narrow eight-year-old face, grinned from a school photo in the center of the snowman's belly.

"Pretty cute," she said.

"If you like Bugs Bunny."

She smiled. "All kids go through that stage."

"This is my favorite shot. No teeth showing." He took a photo from the fireplace mantel and handed it to her. "That's my dad."

The picture recorded a skinny, uncertain seven-year-old Ian in midjump off the diving board. His dad waited below in the water, arms stretched up.

"Were you scared?"

"Terrified. But Dad said I could do it. I believed him." And he would rather have drowned than disappoint his dad.

Memories washed over him of the strong, quiet father who'd taught him everything he knew about being a man. From how to fix a flat tire to how to pray, Dad had been a terrific role model. Sometimes he wondered how he'd been so lucky to have Robert Carpenter for a dad. Christmas wasn't the same without him.

"How long did you say he's been gone?" Gretchen asked.

"Two years. I'd give anything if we could have one more Christmas together."

"I'm sorry. I know how hard it is to lose someone you love."

He touched her fingers where they curled around the picture frame. "I know you do. And I'm sorry, too."

Though she seldom mentioned Maddy, this first Christmas without her sister had to hurt like mad. Suddenly, he was glad he'd invited her.

He gently reclaimed the photo, returning it to the mantel as his mother bustled into the living room.

Cheeks pink from the oven, eyes dancing with happiness, she said, "If you like pictures, I've got albums full of the things. Ian was so cute, we took zillions."

As if that wasn't obvious from the wall and table decor.

Ian rolled his eyes and groaned. "Mom."

She flapped her hand at him. "Well, you were."

Gretchen apparently enjoyed torturing him. Either that, or she thought the secrets of Isaiah House resided in his childhood. "I'd love to look at your albums."

His mother beamed. Score one for Gretchen. "After dinner we'll dig them out. Come on now, everything's ready."

They filed into the dining room where his mother had outdone herself. Gleaming silver and china, steaming vegetables, glazed turkey breast with Mama's special Jezebel sauce and yeasty, hot bread filled the lovely, old table. Mom was in her element.

As Ian held her chair, Gretchen looked back at him. "This looks wonderful."

So did she. And she smelled good, too. Even with the tantalizing scents of Mom's home cooking, Ian couldn't miss the unmistakable lemony fragrance that was Gretchen.

"A little different than the soup kitchen, huh?"

Ian moved to seat his mother and then took the place at the head of the table, stomach growling in anticipation. He hadn't had Mom's home cooking in months. In his line of work, meals were grab-and-go.

"Ian, will you please ask the blessing?" his mother asked.

Elbows on either side of his plate, hands folded at his chin, he offered thanks for the meal, for the company, and most of all for mankind's greatest Christmas gift ever. Inside he prayed that Gretchen would witness the true meaning of Christmas in his mother's home and grow hungry to know the Savior as he did. He also prayed that she would see him as he really was, a simple man of faith doing the best he could to make a difference. He needed to stop the lingering worry that she might yet discredit Isaiah House on television.

"Amen."

The word was echoed by his mother. Then Gretchen also softly murmured, "Amen."

She opened her eyes and looked at him, smiling a little as if sensing—and enjoying—his surprise. Her green gaze held his for several seconds before she glanced down.

Something in that tiny smile got to him. A warmth spread through his chest, filling him. He reached for his iced tea and swigged the cold sweetness past the disquiet.

His mother, a master of polite conversation and Southern hospitality kept small talk flowing easily around the dinner table. Though Ian protested and made groaning noises, she filled Gretchen's ear with his childhood antics. At the same time, she also found ways to draw their guest out. In that short dinner, Ian discovered more about the reporter's work and her life than he'd learned since they'd met.

Gretchen seemed comfortable in his mother's home. So comfortable and warm and friendly that Ian would have a hard time convincing Mom that Gretchen was a hard-nosed barracuda who ate charities and politicians for breakfast.

Midway through the meal the telephone rang. The sudden noise startled Margot. She jumped and gasped, a hand going to her lips. Ian tossed his napkin aside and pushed back. "Stay put, Mom. I'll get it."

"No, no." She leaped up from the table and waved him off. "It's probably my friend Theresa wanting to brag on some new gadget her daughter brought from Chicago. Get the pie out of the fridge. I'll be right back."

As soon as she left the room Ian went to the refrigerator. Over one shoulder, he called, "Pecan, pumpkin, chocolate cream or coconut?"

"You've got to be kidding." Gretchen rose and came into the kitchen. "You're not kidding."

Ian refused to think about how close she was or how tempted he was to remain here with his head in the fridge forever.

"Mom goes a little overboard when I come to visit."

"Who's going to eat all those?" she asked in wonder.

"We are. What we don't eat today, she'll cover with foil and send home with us."

"Your mom is amazing."

"Yes, she is. And I'm a blessed man." He patted his belly. "So where should we begin?"

She pointed to the chocolate. "I haven't had that since I was small."

"Chocolate cream loaded with Mom's golden meringue coming right up." With a flourish he swept the pie from the shelf, mouth watering as he cut three huge slices.

"Was it Theresa?" he asked as Margot returned to the table.

"No."

Her strained, curt tone caught his attention.

Ian frowned, noticing now that she had paled and her fingers trembled as she accepted the saucer of pie from Gretchen.

"Mom, what's wrong? Who was that?"

"No one, honey. A wrong number. That's all."

A wrong number took that long? "Then why are you shaking?"

"Because I'm an old woman. Now, stop fretting."

He didn't like thinking about her age. "Have you been sick again?"

"Don't start fussing, Ian. I'm fine." She rolled her eyes toward Gretchen. "He's such a nag sometimes."

The gentle rebuke was spoken with affection.

"When are you seeing the doctor again?"

"Next Tuesday morning, though there is not a bit of need in it."

"You'll call me afterward?"

"Yes, yes." She'd regained her color and seemed less shaky. "Now eat your pie. It's made from scratch."

They finished dessert with a return to general conversation, but Ian couldn't shake the feeling that something was wrong with his mother. Sure, she was getting up in years, but she had always looked and acted so much younger. He couldn't stand thinking that something serious could be wrong. She was all the family he had left.

As he slid a fork into the rich, creamy pie, he focused his attention on his mother. She chatted away as though nothing had happened, and he hoped his gut instinct had missed the mark this time. Dad was gone. He couldn't bear to lose Mom, too.

Not yet, Lord. Please, not yet.

For as long as he could remember he'd been terrified of losing his parents. As a boy, he'd often dreamed they had disappeared and he couldn't find them. Even now, when he was stressed the dream still came. Then the other nightmare would take hold, and he'd wake up shaking and cold and crying like a baby. He hated the dreams. Hated to even think about them.

Automatically, he touched the pocket of his slacks and felt the fish key chain through the thick fabric. He had never understood why the little metal trinket brought such comfort. He only knew that it did.

"Ian." Gretchen's voice broke into his thoughts. He

looked up to find both women clearing the table, the meal apparently over. His plate was empty, though he didn't recall tasting his favorite pie.

He scraped his chair away from the table.

"I'll do KP." Anything to shake the dread that had settled over him.

"And I'll help," Gretchen offered. She took Margot's apron from the back of the chair and tied it around her narrow waist.

Ian nudged Margot away from the sink. "You take a rest. You cooked, we'll clean."

"I'll go put on some Christmas carols." His mom shook a finger at him and grinned. "And dig out those picture albums."

"Retribution for my boyhood misdeeds," he muttered and was rewarded by Gretchen's giggle.

In no time the kitchen was clean and they settled on the couch with fat, fragrant mugs of spiced tea and Margot's memory books spread out on the coffee table.

Ian figured he might as well go with the flow and let his mother show off their family. She was determined. And from her sly maneuvering to seat Gretchen in the center with him on the left, he suspected she was up to a little matchmaking, as well.

"This is the time Ian broke his arm." She tapped a photo of him in a cast. "Scared me half to death when the school called and said he was hurt."

Gretchen turned her head toward him. The movement stirred her perfume. "What happened?"

"As I recall, Melinda Harris dared me to jump out of the swing."

Her eyes crinkled. "Melinda Harris?"

"Third grade femme fatale. I would have jumped off the Empire State Building for her."

"Did she fall madly in love with you after this great sacrifice?"

He gave an exaggerated sigh of defeat, letting his shoulders droop. "No, she moved to Tennessee before I could even show off my cast. I was heartbroken, let me tell you."

"He was such a sweet boy," Margot said. "All the little girls were crazy for him."

Gretchen grinned at his discomfort. "I'll just bet they were."

"Actually, they liked me because my mom packed homemade cookies in my backpack to share in the cafeteria."

"Oh, go on with that." Margot flipped the page and pointed. "Here's his sixth birthday party. Look at all those kids around him."

"Again, Mom. I had cake to share. And ice cream."

His mother pushed the air with one hand and kept turning pages, pointing out the well-documented chronicle of his childhood.

"What's this one?" Gretchen touched a picture of him in a hospital bed, pale as the sheets, an IV running into his arm. Colorful balloons and teddy bears lined the bedside table and nightstand. "Were you sick?"

"Meningitis, wasn't it, Mom?" His memories from that time in the hospital were nothing more than vague, disturbed impressions.

"Oh, yes. My poor darling." Margot shook her head

as she studied the photo. "He was so sick. All because of an earache. His temperature shot up to 105 and he was limp as a dishrag. For days he didn't know a thing. Just lay there with fever coming off him in waves, whimpering like a puppy. We prayed the house down, I'll tell you. Scared out of our minds that we'd lose him after waiting all those years to get him."

"I don't remember too much about it." He'd only been five.

Margot reached across and patted his knee. "And a mercy that is, too, son."

"Except for the ice cream." And the fear that his parents would leave him in the hospital and not come back because he was so much trouble. He kept that memory to himself. "Dad brought ice cream, six different flavors."

"Your daddy was so distraught. He thought if he tempted you with enough foods, you'd eat something. Bless his heart." She gave a little shiver. "Turn the page, Gretchen. I only keep those pictures as a reminder of how much God has blessed me, of how He answered our prayers for a child and then brought that child through a life-threatening illness. He's been so good to us."

His mother's comment touched a soft place in Ian's heart. All his life, she'd talked like that, calling him a blessing. He wondered why he had so much trouble accepting the compliment.

If Margot's talk of God bothered Gretchen, she didn't let it show. She continued to turn the pages of the album, asking questions, making comments and sharing an occasional laugh at Ian's antics.

Page after page went by, mostly of him and his

friends. Pets, camps, clubs. His parents and the small clutch of extended family that arrived on holidays. The marching band and later the jazz ensemble at church. In cap and gown at graduation with his parents standing proudly beside him. Mom hadn't missed a single photo op of her little boy.

When they came to the final page, Gretchen sat back against the couch cushions with a smile. "You're right, Mrs. Carpenter. Ian was a pretty cute kid, but where are his baby pictures?"

The heaviness that had dissipated during the walk down memory lane, suddenly returned in full force. Did he have a baby book?

The phone rang. His mother jumped, knocking an album to the floor. Pictures scattered everywhere.

"I'll get that," Ian said firmly and made a dive for the phone before his mother could collect herself. This was the second time she'd overreacted to a ringing telephone.

"Hello?" He listened briefly then held the receiver out. "It's Theresa."

Nothing sinister or worrisome about his mother's best friend, but Margot's hand trembled as she took the phone. And she wouldn't look at him.

This wasn't like her. Why was she acting so strange?

He thought about the phone call a while back informing him that his mother had fainted at the health club. Had she had more of those episodes? Was she afraid one of her friends would call and tell him?

It scared him to think his mother might be sick and

hiding the fact out of love. Or that something else was going on in her life and she didn't want him to know.

Ian's stomach started to hurt. Something was wrong, and he had a bad feeling that he wouldn't be happy with the answer.

Chapter Nine

Gretchen had lived in New Orleans long enough to be immune to street performers. Most of them, anyway. The only one that could hold her attention hadn't noticed she was here yet.

Jackson Square was alive with entertainers this Saturday afternoon, a prelude to next month's revelry of Mardi Gras. Jugglers, magicians, dancers, mimes and musicians strutted their stuff for tourist dollars. Ian was in their midst.

Lost in the music, the preacher's body swayed, and one foot tapped rhythm to the lively sound of his gospel saxophone. The joyous melody was enough to attract a handful of spectators, including herself.

She hadn't intended to see him today, but since Christmas, she found herself at the mission more and more—and not on official business. Her relationship with Ian had changed and she wasn't sure what to do about it.

She'd had a great time with him and his feisty,

friendly mother in Baton Rouge. For a while she'd even forgotten her grief at spending Christmas without Maddy. And at the end of a near-perfect day, Ian had surprised her with a completely unexpected Christmas gift, a pair of tickets to an upcoming car show.

Since then she'd had a hard time focusing on her work and an even harder time remembering that Ian was a minister.

Okay, so she was attracted to him. Big-time.

Just as she was attracted to the perfect family life he'd lived. If she and Maddy had been lucky enough to have had a normal suburban upbringing like Ian's, perhaps her sister would still be alive.

Gretchen shifted positions, her back protesting from the extended contact with tree bark. Such thoughts were useless now. She couldn't bring Maddy back. She'd finally come to terms with the fact that she had wanted to blame Ian for Maddy's death. Maybe she still did, but she liked him, too, a conflict she had yet to resolve.

This afternoon, however, she was once again here on business.

Marian Jacobs was now pressing for an independent audit of Isaiah House finances. Gretchen thought Ian should know. She also wanted his reaction.

To tell the truth, the councilwoman's annoying vendetta against Isaiah House and other charities was beginning to grow tiresome. The press continued to eat it up but Gretchen wondered if Jacobs's complaints were political maneuvering rather than truly trying to serve the public interest.

One thing Gretchen knew for sure, she no longer

wanted to find any wrongdoing here. Ian's work mattered. Kids received help at Isaiah House. She'd seen that firsthand.

But as a respected journalist she had to go where the stories were. This was her job. To do less would jeopardize her reputation and possibly even her career.

Some ministers *did* dip into the funds for personal expenditures. It happened. Though, to this point, she'd spent enough time with Ian to know he wasn't a big spender. He didn't own a house or even a nice car. He wasn't into drugs as she'd once suspected. And he apparently wasn't into parties or gambling.

The only thing other than the mission that he spent money on was shoes. But he gave away far more than he kept. She had a snazzy pair of three-inch rhinestone heels to prove it. The man simply liked to buy shoes. A weird vice for a guy, yes, but definitely not a big expenditure, and even there he claimed personal assets. After visiting his mother's home, she believed him.

The ever-surfacing accusations didn't fit her insider view of Ian or of Isaiah House. But she'd started this series and now she had no choice but to follow through.

So here she was, spending her afternoon on the streets of the French Quarter. According to the doleful Roger, Ian was "playing a preachin' gig."

In his usual jeans, athletic shoes and ball cap the Isaiah House director looked more like a college student than a clergyman. The only thing about him that appeared the least bit religious was his T-shirt. The name and address of Isaiah House was on the back. On the front was a paraphrase of Isaiah 58:9, "When you cry for help, He will say: Here I am."

By now the scriptures were as familiar to her as his phone number. Early in her investigation she'd studied the verses over and over in an effort to understand what made Ian Carpenter tick.

At the end of Ian's song, applause sounded and a number of people came forward to drop bills and coins into a box marked Isaiah House. She found it curious that Ian resorted to raising funds in such an unorthodox manner. But then, everything about this preacher was different from any she'd ever encountered, including Brother Gordon.

The mission depended upon donations. Why should she be surprised that Ian used his considerable musical talents to raise money?

An ancient man in a ragged camouflage jacket and stained straw hat shuffled forward. From the looks of him, Gretchen couldn't imagine the man having money to donate. He and Ian exchanged a few words that Gretchen couldn't hear.

With one foot she pushed away from the tree and moved closer. The old man reeked of alcohol.

"Nice horn you got there, son. A Mark IV, ain't she?"

With the same practiced care she'd seen him use before, Ian turned the saxophone to a horizontal position. The sunlight glinted off the glossy, engraved brass. "Yes, sir. She is."

"Figured. Don't hear that quality every day."

"You play." Ian's words were a statement.

"I used to blow a tune now and then." No one could

miss the longing in the man's watery old eyes. "Even had a Selmer once."

Ian extended the vintage saxophone. The mother-of-pearl key covers gleamed iridescent. "Will you play for us?"

Gretchen couldn't believe it. She knew how special that vintage sax was to Ian. Surely, he must smell the liquor. But if he did, he didn't let his aversion show.

The man, gaunt and wobbly, hesitated. Ian smiled that gentle, mesmerizing smile of his, and nodded encouragement. "We'd be honored."

Bloodshot eyes took on a dreamy, faraway expression. From his pants pockets, the man removed a mouthpiece. "I still carry this. Don't know why, ain't got my horn no more."

With shaky, gnarled fingers that appeared incapable of manipulating the rows of shiny keys, the old gentleman accepted the instrument. Taking exquisite care, as if the horn was a fragile butterfly, he turned it this way and that, checking the keys, changing the mouthpiece, stroking the gleaming bell. He handled the instrument with the same care she'd seen Ian take.

Then he lifted the beautiful old Selmer toward Heaven and began to play.

A hush fell over the onlookers as they exchanged startled glances. The man's stooped shoulders straightened. With each honeyed note, he seemed to become taller, younger, steadier. Any sign of inebriation disappeared in the powerful, practiced exercise of giving life to a piece of glittering, lacquered brass.

In quiet respect, Ian folded his legs beneath him and

sat down on the concrete at the other musician's feet. Gretchen moved to sit beside him.

She started down, tilted the slightest bit and was forced to place a hand on Ian's shoulder for balance. Strong muscles rippled beneath her fingers. Ian glanced up, face alight with welcome. Gretchen's undisciplined heart flip-flopped. She quickly removed her hand and diverted her attention to the street musician. But she couldn't forget the manly strength or the tender expression in Ian's eyes.

Something was happening to her. And whatever it was, Ian was responsible.

A rich, haunting melody reverberated over the square. More listeners drifted close.

In one part of her mind, she realized that the saxophonist was excellent. But the main focus of her thoughts was the man beside her. They sat close enough that if she swayed to the music, her arm would touch his. Like a teenager with a crush, she was tempted to do it.

She held herself rigid, afraid her own body would betray her. She couldn't put her confidence in a preacher. She shouldn't like one, either. Yet, Ian was different in so many ways.

Confused and wanting to escape a problem she couldn't seem to resolve, Gretchen closed her eyes and listened to the impromptu concert. Ian played well. But this ragged old man was masterful. In seconds, goose bumps prickled her skin.

"Incredible."

She didn't know she'd spoken aloud until Ian said, "Yeah."

She looked his way, saw that he wore the same rapt, dreamy look that had overtaken the guest saxophonist.

"You knew he was this good," she murmured.

"Suspected."

And as one musician to another, Ian must have felt the hunger in the man, had sensed his desire to play even though he no longer owned an instrument. So, out of kindness he'd handed over his prized saxophone to a half-drunk street bum who doubtless carried a sad secret.

When the music died away, applause thundered and dollars whispered against coins as they were tossed into the box. The old man, who'd been as forlorn as an orphaned kitten, now stood proud as he accepted the accolades. Over and over, he tilted his head in thanks, a tiny smile pulling the corners of his mouth.

Tears threatened as Gretchen's heart twisted. Ian had done that for him. He'd given the battered old musician an admiring audience and restored his pride, if only for a little while.

Ian didn't move for several long seconds after the music died. He let the man soak up the much-deserved attention. Finally, the saxophone was returned. The wobble, which had disappeared during the brief concert, returned to the old musician's fingers.

"Sweet horn. Thank you, son."

"No, sir. Thank you." Ian stepped closer, and words meant only for the two men were exchanged.

Around them the onlookers began to drift away. Ian hadn't preached one word.

From her seat on the hard, sun-heated concrete, Gretchen pondered her puzzling preacher. He was here to preach, but hadn't. He was here to play and yet he'd given up his audience. He hadn't even done a pitch to collect money for the mission.

Ian Carpenter was driving her crazy.

As much as she didn't relish the job, she would tell him about the audit, get his reaction and get out of here. Being attracted to a preacher was the dumbest thing she'd done in a long time.

Shaking her head at her own foolishness, she pushed up from the ground and dusted the seat of her capris.

Even after what had happened to her and Maddy as kids, she was still too weak to resist a smooth-talking preacher. Pathetic. Women like her must have some perverse need to be controlled.

This was ridiculous.

With a rapid change of direction, she started toward the outrageously expensive parking lot, leaving Ian and the man to talk. Ian hadn't invited her here. She wasn't some groupie who needed to hang around and talk to him. She was a professional businesswoman here only to ask questions about the audit, not to ogle a good-looking preacher. She could do this interview by phone.

Half a block into her resolve, Ian jogged up beside her. "Wanna grab some lunch?"

"I've already had lunch." She thrust her chin into the air, intending to sound dismissive. Then she noticed he carried the saxophone but not the money box. "You gave your money to that man."

One shoulder twitched. "He earned it. Not me."

Gretchen stopped in the middle of the sidewalk.

She'd seen Brother Gordon work the crowds for an hour at a time, pumping them for more money while she and the other followers collected the cash for him. Not once, had she ever seen him give any of it away.

Time after time, she'd seen Ian do things for others and receive nothing in return.

"How can you support the mission if you give your donations away?"

"God supplies the money. He can handle it."

He was so steady, so confident of who he was and what his place in life was all about. If only she could have one moment of feeling that way. Instead she spent her entire life trying to prove a point and only ended up emptier and more uncertain.

"What a weird thing to say."

Ian laughed, a loud ringing bark that both embarrassed and amused her.

"It's not funny. How you can expect the mission to thrive when you're so cavalier about your funds. Are you aware that Marian Jacobs is requesting an audit?"

The words flew out before she was ready. So much for subtlety.

Ian's humor died away. "Of Isaiah House?"

"I received a tip this morning. Are they going to find anything?"

They stood beneath an enormous live oak, its leaves whispering secrets to each other.

"What do you think?" he asked quietly.

"I'm asking, Ian. I need to know."

"And I need to know you have enough confidence in me not to have to ask."

Frustrated and conflicted, she looked up through the leaves and dappled sunshine.

"You know I have to follow this story to the end."

"Which comes first, Gretchen, your job or a friend?"

"That's not fair."

"It *is* fair. You know who I am. Stop waiting for me to turn into the bogeyman."

Brother Gordon had.

When she didn't answer, his shoulders rose and fell in frustration. "Look, Gretchen, I don't care about the audit. But I'd like to know you believe in me."

"I want to." But she was so scared of being fooled again.

Confusion boiled inside like a geyser waiting to erupt. She liked him. She was attracted to him. But he was a preacher, and she didn't dare believe a preacher. Even Ian.

Did she?

Chapter Ten

He should have called first.

Palms damp with uncertainty, Ian pulled into the single parking spot outside Gretchen's apartment complex.

What if Gretchen had changed her mind about tonight?

He killed the motor and squinted up the steps to the door marked 12B.

The woman was getting under his skin in the worst way. Her inside knowledge about a possible audit was no big deal. What really hurt was that Gretchen thought he'd done something illegal to merit the action.

He examined that, rolled it over in his head. Why should he be upset? She'd thought the worst of him since the beginning. But that was before the barracuda had become a real woman, an appealing woman. They had worked side by side to help the needy. They'd had fun together. He'd thought they were finally past the suspicion and raw distrust. Apparently, they weren't.

And that hurt.

His feelings aside, if Gretchen was ever going to find her way back to the Lord, she had to learn to trust.

He didn't give a rip about the audit. Other than the unsolved theft of petty cash, Isaiah House's finances were in impeccable order. Roger would have told him if anything was amiss.

But if he was honest, which he always tried to be, he needed Gretchen to have confidence in him. He liked her. After all their time together, the least she could do was trust him in return.

Gathering his courage, he shoved the van door open. Just then Gretchen stepped out on the landing. Ian's stomach took a nosedive. He grabbed his ball cap from the seat, shoved it on and jogged to the stairwell.

Tonight was the car and truck show, and he'd looked forward to the evening since Christmas. After the confrontation in the Square, he hadn't been sure she'd still want to go.

Not that this was a date, mind you. He knew better than to think that way about an unbeliever.

But he wished he could.

He stopped dead still on the top stair, slam-dunked by the revelation. He, a clergyman, was having serious thoughts about a woman who not only distrusted him but also distrusted God.

Now, that was a reality check if ever there was one.

He started on up the steps.

He was a minister first and last. End of story.

The Superdome was packed.

After more than an hour of wandering the floor to

look at brightly painted trucks, shining chrome wheels and jacked-up, oversize vehicles, Ian realized how silly he was to pretend Gretchen was any other lost soul he wanted to save. He wanted her to renew her faith, all right, but his motives bordered on pure self-interest.

Man, was he a dandy preacher, or what?

Looking far too pretty in a short turquoise overjacket that turned her eyes to emeralds, she hadn't said a word about the audit or the unpleasant exchange they'd had in the Quarter.

She folded a piece of pink cotton candy and stuffed it into her mouth. "So how do you like the car show? Great, huh?"

"The best." And he wasn't kidding. When they didn't discuss the mission or her job, they had a blast. In pretend weariness he leaned against a truck wheel at least three feet taller than himself. "Fun, but exhausting."

"I thought the great Reverend Ian never tired." Her eyes sparkled with orneriness as she teased him with the disliked title. "Preaching, praying and counseling all day, prowling the streets all night."

"And don't forget, fending off troublesome television reporters." He winced, regretting the slip of the tongue. Her work was the last thing he wanted to mention.

"There's always that. Exhausting, I'm sure." She ripped another piece of candy from the cone. "Here. Have an energy boost."

She poked the sugary confection at his mouth and let the opportunity to probe slide right past.

The moment her fingertips touched his lips, thoughts of the audit disappeared and Ian was right back to thinking about her. Noticing the curve of her sugary, moist lips. Wondering what it would be like to kiss her.

Stop right there, preacher.

The warning in his head buzzed loud and serious. Time to back off and think about something else. Anything else.

He took one giant step backward and looked around. Hot dogs, shrimp, butter-dripping cinnamon rolls. Food beckoned from every direction.

"Let's grab a real bite," he said.

"What?" she asked in mock seriousness. "You want something more substantial than cotton candy?"

"Yes. I do. Good old-fashioned health food. You know, a hot dog with cheese and chili."

"And a big bag of potato chips?"

"Now you're talking."

At the counter, Gretchen succumbed to the lure of golden fried shrimp while he focused on the chili dog. They got their orders and chose a place with tables away from the worst noise of the ongoing rock concert located at the far end of the building.

As he placed his hot, brimming full paper boat on the table and sat down, Ian raised his voice. "If that gets any louder, the roof is going to come off."

Gretchen laughed, energized by the noisy, crowded show. "Admit it, Ian. You want to get up there and jam with them."

"Think they could use a gospel saxophone?"

This time they both laughed. The hard, pumping rock music was about as far from Ian's cool jazz style as any music could be.

"I'll bet you could play with them. You're good enough."

The compliment warmed him, but he didn't take it too seriously.

"That sounds like something my mom would say."

"Your mom's a smart lady." She bit into a jumbo shrimp. "This is good. How's your hot dog?"

"Can't compare to a Lucky Dog, but it's okay."

"I knew you'd say that." She always teased him about being addicted to the street vendor hot dogs in the Quarter. "How's your mother doing?"

"According to Mom? Or the truth?"

She blinked at him over the rim of her Coke cup. "Is something wrong?"

"Her doctor ordered some tests."

"Bad news?"

"I hope not. But she is seventy-one and her heartbeat is irregular. The doctor ordered a stress test to see if that could cause the 'little spells' she's been having."

"Didn't you say she'd only had one of those?"

"She didn't tell me about the others."

"Trying to protect her baby boy?"

It was exactly what his mother would do, had always done. Hide the truth from him, so he wouldn't worry. She'd done the same thing with Dad.

"If my mother has something wrong with her heart, I need to know, whether she likes it or not."

"Are you going up to Baton Rouge?"

"During the tests?" His gut clenched with dread. "Got to."

"Worried?"

Ian scraped his straw in and out of the plastic lid. Sure he was worried. Worse than worried. He was scared out of his mind. "Mom has been my rock for a long time. Now I have to be hers."

With the whisper-touch of her fingers, Gretchen stopped the nervous jiggling of his straw. "Would you like some company?"

Ian studied her sincere expression, a dozen conflicting emotions going off in his head. "Are you offering?"

"I am."

He knew he should refuse, but he wanted her company.

"I'd like that."

"Good. It's settled then." With a pleased expression, she returned to the last few shrimp and fries.

Ian missed her touch the second she moved.

Boy, was he in trouble. The woman had him in a tangle. He had never before had a problem maintaining a professional reserve from women who did not share his faith. But Gretchen had shoved right through that wall in nothing flat. He wanted to be with her. He wanted to know her better. He wanted to be more than a news story.

And he wasn't sure what to do about it.

They ate without talking for a while. Engines roared. Rock music vibrated the walls. Ian stewed.

If he was getting emotionally involved—and he was pretty sure he was—he needed answers to some serious questions.

He knew Gretchen's favorite color, her birthday and what made her laugh. But he still didn't know where she stood spiritually. She was so prickly about the topic, he'd been afraid to go there lest he drive her away.

Some minister he was.

Finally, he dragged a napkin across his mouth, took a sip of watery Coke, and said, "I want to ask you something."

She paused, a shrimp dangling from grease-shined fingers. "Uh-oh. Sounds serious."

"It is." Hands steepled, he bounced thumb knuckles against his chin. If he didn't do this right, he risked losing her altogether, both personally and spiritually. Yet he couldn't wait any longer to have this conversation.

Gretchen popped the shrimp into her mouth and chewed, thoughtful. Wariness crept into gorgeous green eyes. "Okay."

"If I ask you something personal, will you tell me?"

She leaned back in her chair, on alert. He could practically see the wheels turning in her head. "Will you do the same for me?"

"Yes. You can even go first." To calm the jitters dancing in his belly, he fed them a potato chip and braced for more questions about the mission or the audit.

"Why aren't you married?"

Considering his thoughts of the last few minutes, the question bore a certain irony.

"Easy." He shrugged. "So far, no one has wanted to marry me."

One finely arched eyebrow shot up. "I don't believe that."

"Scout's honor."

Even the Scouting oath didn't convince her. "No girlfriends at all? Not even one?"

"I didn't say that." His humor faded. "I said, none that would marry me."

Gretchen was on the mood change like cheese on a cracker. "Some cheating girlfriend broke your heart."

He tried to joke away the revelation. "You always were too smart for my own good. She didn't cheat, but she did break my heart."

"What happened?"

He was long over the breakup, but Tamma wasn't a topic he enjoyed discussing.

He pointed his soda straw at his companion. "Wasn't this supposed to be *one* personal question?"

She stuck her chin out and made a face. "Same question. Now I'm asking for details."

"Newswomen." He shook his head in mock dismay. "Always have to have details."

She tapped him playfully on the arm. "All women want details. Competition is fierce out there."

Competition? Though he probably shouldn't, he liked the sound of that.

"When I was in college, there was this girl. Tamma. She was perfect."

This time Gretchen raised both eyebrows.

"Yep. A perfect pastor's wife. We dated seriously for more than a year. I proposed."

"And she turned you down?"

"Actually, she said yes until I decided to open Isaiah House." He rotated the thick paper cup between his palms. "You see, Tamma and I had different ideas about ministry. She wanted us to pastor a huge congregation in an affluent area with lots of social activities and all the other trimmings."

"And you couldn't do that."

He spread his arms wide. "Can you see me in that kind of position?"

"No. I can't. They'd throw you out for wearing tattered ball caps in the pulpit."

"Or tennis shoes?" He wiggled his foot, accidentally brushing hers beneath the table. She didn't bother to move away. "Isaiah House is my calling. I'm where I belong. And Tamma is where she belongs."

"She found her a big-time pastor?"

"One of my college buddies stepped right in as soon as we broke up."

Gretchen reached across the table and squeezed his hand. "Sorry I opened that old wound."

"You didn't. I'm happy with my choice. No regrets." But if she'd hold his hand again, he might tell her more sad stories.

In reality, he'd hurt for a long time after his breakup with Tamma, had even questioned his calling, but the last three years of making a difference had healed him.

"Okay, then." She diddled with the one shrimp remaining on her plate. "Your turn."

"You won't like the question."

Gretchen's pulse picked up. A funny feeling jittered in her belly. She had a good idea where Ian was headed with his questions.

"Then don't ask it."

He tilted back in the folding chair and crossed his

arms over a T-shirt bearing the slogan *Life Is Short, Pray Hard*. “A deal is a deal.”

“May I ask what it pertains to first?”

His long pause made her even more nervous. Finally, in that gentle baritone, he said, “Your faith.”

Defenses shot up around her like a force field. Fireworks went off in her head. “I believe in God.”

“You believe in Him, but you don’t like Him much. Why, Gretchen? What made you so bitter?”

Gretchen’s shrimp soured in her stomach. She twisted her soda straw round and round while a booming loudspeaker and the scent of fried vendor foods invaded their space.

She liked Ian. A lot. She wanted to be open and honest with him. But how did she explain the nightmare she and Maddy had experienced to a man whose suburban life had been nearly perfect?

“I can’t talk about this here.” Something so personal and ugly required privacy.

Disappointment filtered through Ian’s expression, but to his credit he didn’t argue. “Later then?”

She pushed back from the table and scooped up her trash. “I’m ready to go when you are.”

He reached out and caught her arm, stopping her sudden burst of nervous energy. “Did I upset you?”

“No.” She relented. “Yes. But you’re right. We do need to talk about this.”

She wanted him to understand why she would always be suspicious. Why she would always second-guess every ministry, every spiritual decision. She had to for her own protection and her own sanity.

Releasing her arm, Ian helped bus the table before leading the way from the crowded dome into the parking lot.

The February night was cool and a slight breeze carried the scent of the Mississippi into downtown. The moon hovered like a benevolent face in the inky sky.

"Cold?" Ian asked.

She wanted to say yes in case he was tempted to put his arm around her. "My jacket is enough."

"The van's this way, I think." As natural as could be, he took her hand and tugged her close to his side.

At her age, she'd thought herself past that soaring sense of delight at holding hands with a member of the opposite sex. She'd been wrong.

After wondering if the man would ever make a move, the warm strength of that hand wrapped around hers was about the most satisfying romance she'd ever experienced. She, the strong, confident career woman who'd taken care of herself since she was thirteen years old felt fragile, protected.

When they reached the vehicle, he opened the passenger door, then bracketed her waist with both hands and helped her inside.

Seated, she turned to look at him. "If you keep this up, I'll tell you *all* my secrets."

Face shadowed by the security lights, Ian looked mysterious and oh-so attractive. He touched her cheek, his gentle voice going deep and gravelly. "Then get ready to tell me everything."

Gretchen's heart fluttered.

When they were on the road winding through the

busy streets of the city Ian slipped a CD into the player. Across the bench seat he once again found her hand.

"Want to know my favorite thing about tonight? Besides being with you."

Though the words thrilled her, she playfully rolled her eyes. "Sweet talker. You really are after my secrets."

His teeth flashed white in the dash lights. "We didn't have one discussion tonight about the mission or the TV station."

She noticed how he carefully avoided mentioning the prospect of an audit.

"I don't want to believe anything bad about you, Ian. I meant that."

He glanced at her, electric eyes serious. "I'm glad."

"I want a life outside my career."

"So do I," he said. "Though sometimes I have trouble separating the two."

"I can see that. Your faith *is* your job, but it's also who you are."

"Then maybe you can understand why it's so important for me to know where you stand spiritually."

Yes, she understood, and in doing so she accepted the fact that something was happening between them. Regardless of her job or Ian's naysayers, regardless of her fear of being controlled by another preacher, she needed to find out where this thing with Ian was headed.

While the stereo played a soaring Celine Dion classic, Gretchen pulled away to stare out at the passing cars. Ian was wise enough to stay silent and let her do this in her own way.

Finally, hands clasped tightly in her lap, she blew out

the breath she'd been holding. "I'm going to tell you something, Ian. But first you have to promise not to judge me for what happened. Okay?"

He glanced at her. Passing headlights flickered over his concerned face. "I'd never do that."

She hoped not. "You don't know what I'm going to say."

"Anything that you've done or haven't done won't change the way I feel about you."

The precise, careful phrasing gave her pause. She studied him for several thrilled and frightened heartbeats. She was no fool. All the signs had been pointing in this direction for a while now. Ian cared for her. And the revelation gave her the confidence to tell him what she'd never been able to fully share with anyone but Maddy.

"All right, then. Hold on to your ball cap."

Jokingly, he clapped one hand on top of his head, but his eyes were serious as they flickered from the road to her and back again. "Ready when you are."

"I've lived a strange life, Ian. Very strange." She hesitated, heart pounding louder than the music at the Superdome. The shame and embarrassment of her past pressed against her rib cage. Everything in her screamed not to say another word. What would a steady, sensible man like Ian think?

"You can tell me anything, Gretchen. Anything."

That was all she needed to hear.

On a rush of courage, she blurted, "Maddy and I grew up in a religious commune."

Chapter Eleven

"A commune?" Ian struggled to keep his reply composed and his eyes on the road. If he overreacted to her strange declaration, she might stop talking altogether. And he had a feeling he was about to understand Gretchen in an entirely new way. "Must have been an interesting way to grow up."

"What a diplomatic way of saying we were weird." When he started to protest she waved him off. "No, don't apologize. We *were* weird. But you have to understand something. Maddy and I were kids. What did we know? Mother and Dad were happy, we were happy. Most of the time."

He knew about communes. Unfortunately, he didn't know anything good. "What went wrong?"

"We were taught to believe that our leader, Brother Gordon, was the right hand of God, maybe even God himself." She gave a bitter laugh. "He wasn't."

She fell silent, reluctance written all over her. Whatever had happened in that commune had left a deep wound.

"When I look back at my life now," she said, "the deception seems so clear. But at the time, all I knew was the Family of Love. The Family was everything, Brother Gordon was our prophet, and anyone who did not believe that was doomed for all eternity. His word was law."

"Pretty scary stuff to a kid."

"Tell me about it. Once I cried for a Barbie doll and was brought before the congregation as an example of worldliness and disobedience. My punishment was isolation. Days and days of isolation while I wrote and rewrote the mantra of obedience. Believe me, after that, I meekly accepted whatever I was given."

"What was wrong with a kid having a Barbie doll?"

"Oh, the doll wasn't the problem. Other girls had them, but Brother Gordon had preordained the purchases. They were his idea. As the benevolent prophet, he alone decided what we could and could not have. And one thing we were never allowed to have was a will of our own."

Ian's mouth quirked. "I can't see that working too well with you."

"It didn't, obviously, though the Family tried to help 'free' me from my rebellious ways."

"Gretchen, this is sounding a lot like a cult."

"We *were* a cult, Ian. A cult. How could my parents have been so terribly deceived?"

By now, they'd reached Gretchen's apartment. Ian pulled the van into the narrow strip of concrete parking and killed the motor.

"It happens," he said, turning to face her across the long seat. "A lot more than any of us would like to believe. A group starts out with good intentions but somewhere along the way, the leader goes astray, the scripture is twisted, and the fight for control begins."

A security light from the street cast a white glow into the van's interior adding pallor to Gretchen's already pale skin.

"Control. That's exactly the word. Brother Gordon was a master at psychological manipulation. If anyone disagreed with his teachings that person was a gossip causing dissension and divisiveness among the Family." Her lip curled in distaste. "'Because of the Family's great love' we would bring the sinner to the proper understanding and restore him to the faith. As long as he saw things as the group commanded."

She sucked in a long, shuddering breath that told Ian exactly how difficult this was for her. But now that the floodgates had opened, she seemed bent on purging the ugliness hidden inside for so long. He admired her courage.

"I hated my life, Ian, and didn't understand why. I assumed, as I was taught, that I had a wicked soul, that there was something wrong with me. Do you know how confusing that is for a child?"

Ian felt helpless to say anything worthwhile. She'd lived through something he could never understand. "I'm sorry."

"Me, too. Especially for Maddy. She was never able to heal from the psychological damage."

"And you were?"

"I don't know. Maybe not. Maybe I never will. My parents are educated people, Ian, and yet they involved us in a cult. They were so blinded by their devotion to God that they..."

She stopped, her voice filled with unshed tears. Ian could hardly bear to let her go on. No wonder Gretchen struggled with trust. She was as confused about God now as she had been as a child.

He touched her shoulder. "Were your parents blinded by devotion to God? Or to their leader?"

Even though his tone was gentle, the question infuriated her. She jerked away. "It's the same thing, Ian. Don't you get it? It's the same thing."

He wanted to argue the point. But he couldn't. He hadn't lived the nightmare.

Instead, he reached out and pulled both her hands into his. This time she didn't pull away. Whether she wanted to admit it or not, she needed his comfort.

"Those places are notorious for holding on to their followers. How did you get out? When did you know you had to leave?"

She made a harsh, derisive sound in the back of her throat.

"Maddy and I reached what Brother Gordon called the age of accountability. We'd always done everything he said to do up to that point. After all," she said sarcastically, "he was the enlightened leader who guided his flock with a strong, but loving hand. Everyone wanted to please Brother Gordon."

Her lips twisted. "Along with other young girls, we took the oath of loyalty and obedience in an elaborate ceremony. I'll never forget. Maddy and I had long, flowing, white dresses and carried white candles. We were convinced life would get better now that we were leaving childhood behind. We felt so important when Brother Gordon declared us special emissaries of God. Until we found out exactly what that meant."

Ian's jaws tightened. He heard horror stories from the runaways all the time, but nothing angered him as much as the wolves in sheep's clothing that took advantage and used the Lord's name to do it.

"What happened?" he prodded gently.

She didn't look at him again. Instead, she turned his palm over in hers and traced the lines with one finger.

"Faith without works is dead and there will be judgment without mercy if we fail. That's scriptural, Ian. Everything we were taught came from the scripture. So we were taken out into public places. Malls, airports, colleges to recruit new members. At first, we only talked and handed out tracts. But then Brother Gordon began to pressure us to do more. To reach our higher purpose as he called it, by bringing more lost sheep into the fold, along with their worldly goods, of course." She fidgeted. Her voice grew bitter. "That's when Maddy and I realized that the teenage boys never became special emissaries. Only the girls. And we were expected to bring in the young men."

As a man, Ian wanted her to stop. As a minister, he knew she needed to purge all the hurt and guilt.

"In whatever way you could."

"Yes." A slight blush tinged her cheeks. "Our bodies are the temple of the Holy Spirit, according to scripture.

And according to Brother Gordon and the elders, that meant we should use them for the kingdom. This would bring glory to God as well as to us."

"That's a very messed-up interpretation." He didn't want to know if she'd succumbed to this evil deception.

"A lot of people believed it. Still do. But it didn't seem right to me. I prayed and prayed. Finally, I told Mother and Dad. They didn't believe me. Brother Gordon was a holy prophet of God who could do no wrong and I was nothing but an evil-minded, sinful girl."

"What happened?"

"I ran away." A tiny smile broke the strain around her mouth. "Surprised?"

"Not when I put it in perspective. You have a certain empathy with the street kids that most don't have."

"I understand what they're going through. The streets are hard. After a week of being hungry and alone, I went back to the commune." She breathed a self-deprecating huff. "That was a mistake."

"What about Maddy?"

"She didn't run. Maddy was more easily swayed than her stubborn older sister. I never asked her, but I always wondered if..." Her voice trailed away. She bit down on her lip and left the thought unspoken.

"If the drugs were a way to escape what had happened?"

"Yes."

Now he understood all the pointed questions she'd asked him about Isaiah House. She'd been afraid Maddy had fallen into another cult.

"How did you get out?"

"The next time I ran, I convinced Maddy to run with me. Mom and Dad finally woke up after that, though I still think they blame us."

"Why would they blame you?"

"We left the faith. We shattered their utopian dream of the perfect spiritual society. After that our relationship was never the same."

"Maybe they felt guilty for getting you involved in the first place."

"I never considered that." She shook her head. Tears glistened in the corner of her eyes. "They didn't even come to her funeral, Ian. Their own daughter."

Ian ached for her. For her lost innocence. For the loss of her sister. And her parents.

"Christians make mistakes, Gretchen. But most of us sincerely want to follow the precepts of Jesus."

Eyes downcast, she fiddled with the fingers of his left hand.

He slowly made a fist, trapping her fidgety fingers in his. "You don't believe me do you?"

"I guess I don't believe anything anymore."

"If that were true, you wouldn't still be searching."

She looked up, expression yearning. "Am I?"

"Why else would you be so interested in religious groups?"

"I don't want others to be fooled like we were."

"And maybe, just maybe, you're still searching for the answers you couldn't find in the commune."

A new hope glistened through unshed tears. "I suppose you're going to tell me you know the way."

Ian felt trapped. After all she'd experienced in the

cult, even the real truth would be suspect. He couldn't stop the humorless laugh. "Would I sound cultish if I said yes?"

"'Fraid so, Reverend."

He knew better than to go quoting scripture to her, but his brain ran with a dozen that were appropriate. Jesus *was* the truth. The truth that could only be received by faith. God wasn't a hard taskmaster. He was loving and personal.

"All right. I won't tell you. I'll ask you to find out for yourself."

"I've been trying to do that for years."

"Maybe you're looking in all the wrong places."

"Excuse me? Where else, other than churches, should I look?"

"Ministries may *know* the truth, but they *aren't* the truth, if that makes sense."

She rotated one hand back and forth. "Sort of."

"Ministries are run by people. People fail sometimes. God never does." When she started to say something, Ian rushed on, pulse thumping with the crazy hope that he was getting somewhere. "Don't take my word or anyone else's word for who God is and what He expects of you. Read the Bible for yourself. Study it. God is in there. He will reveal Himself to you. He wants you to know Him. And if you know Him, you know the truth."

"I wouldn't have a clue where to begin."

"A suggestion then. Start with the Gospels, Matthew, Mark, Luke and John. Get acquainted with Jesus."

"I guess I can do that."

To Ian, the agreement was a huge step toward victory, and for Gretchen toward ultimate freedom from her spiritual abuse.

"I'm glad you told me."

"You don't think I'm awful?"

"I'm pretty ticked at the Family of Love, but not at you. You're amazing."

She made a funny face. "Which shows how distorted your thinking is."

"Don't do that, Gretchen. You *are* amazing. You not only had the strength to leave the only life you knew, you made a new life. Without anyone's help, you became a successful newswoman."

She touched his cheek. "Thanks for saying that. And for listening. I do feel better in an exhausted sort of way."

"You never told anyone before?"

"Too embarrassed." She took her purse from the floorboard and scooted toward the door. "It's late. I'd better go inside."

Reluctant to part, Ian hopped out of the van and escorted Gretchen to her apartment.

"Want to come in?" she offered, one hand on the doorknob.

Yes.

"Better not." He wanted to take her into his arms, but he wouldn't. He couldn't. "Come by tomorrow? Lunch maybe?"

"Okay." She cupped his cheek again, and any thoughts of not touching her flew out into the night. He took her face into his hands and stared long and hard into the greenest eyes on the planet. A thousand thoughts raced through his mind. But when he feared he might lose the battle and kiss her regardless of his vow not to, she spared him. On tiptoe, she kissed his cheek and stepped back. Ian's hands fell useless through the soft night air to his sides.

"'Night, Ian," she whispered.'

Then she went inside, leaving him standing on the step, both thankful and sorry.

The drive back to the mission gave him plenty of time to think and pray. Tonight, he'd come to understand Gretchen's bitterness and her confusion. He'd also discovered something else. He was falling in love with her.

"Well, Lord, what do you expect me to do now?"

He'd said no to self once before in the situation with Tamma. He didn't know if he could do that this time.

At Isaiah House, he let himself quietly inside and trudged up the stairs to his room. The house was eerily quiet, all the residents long since in bed according to curfew.

Inside his quarters, which consisted of a bedroom and bath, he sat down on the bed and toed off his Adidas.

A grown man really needed a place of his own to live.

The light on his answering machine blinked red. He sighed and rubbed a tired hand over the back of his neck. Probably some mom who couldn't find her kid. Or maybe one of the many kids who had his number. If so, he'd have to put his shoes back on and hit the streets.

The temptation to ignore the message in exchange for a few hours' sleep was strong.

The sense of responsibility was stronger. He remembered Maddy and wished for the hundredth time that she had called him that final night.

Some things couldn't wait until morning.

He pushed Play.

"Ian, this is Tabitha." The day counselor. Must have been a problem today with one of the residents. Listening, he went into the bathroom for his toothbrush. "I meant to leave a note for you, but Emily had a panic attack and I completely forgot. Some man called this afternoon. He said the strangest thing. I didn't think I should wait until tomorrow to tell you."

Something in her tone caught his attention. Ian stepped out of the bathroom to listen more closely.

"He said he thought he might be your brother."

She rattled on about Ian being an only child so the man must have called the wrong number. Ian sank down on the bed and stared at the phone, stomach tight and churning. A bizarre kind of déjà vu swept over him.

His brother? He didn't have a brother.

He shook off the unease and prepared for bed.

Tabitha was right. A wrong number, plain and simple.

But that night, the old childhood nightmare returned in full force. He dreamed of three little boys. One was a scrawny version of himself. They were alone in a dark place, hungry and cold. And in the midst of the nightmare was an older boy who held him when he cried.

Chapter Twelve

Ian was normally a morning person, but not this morning. He awakened disgruntled...and uneasy. Vivid images of last night's dream replayed behind his sleep-puffed eyes.

Stress triggered the dreams. He'd figured that much out long ago. But why this dream? Why three little boys, hungry and alone? Why the terrible aura of impending doom, of some fear he couldn't name even in the light of day?

During chapel the gloom began to lift and by the time he'd conducted Bible study and headed up to his office, he'd managed to shake off the aftereffects and concentrate on the day ahead.

Chrissy had finally agreed to let social services in on her dangerous home situation, a decision that took some of the pressure off him. Two of the boys who had been at Isaiah House the longest were moving out on their own today. Several new volunteers were coming in for the first time. He had plenty to keep his mind occupied.

In his tiny office Ian rummaged in the minifridge, found an icy Mountain Dew and popped the top. A long, bracing swallow of carbonated caffeine jolted him to work.

He made a few last-minute notes in Chrissy's file before phoning his contact in social services. The woman, compassionate as always, knew exactly what to do from here. Chrissy would be in good hands, a fact he'd been trying to drive home for months now. Most teens moved on within sixty to ninety days. Chrissy had been here far longer, fear of her abusive father paralyzing her.

He'd no more than replaced the receiver when the phone rang, lighting up his extension.

"Isaiah House," he answered.

"Is this Ian Carpenter?" a male voice asked.

"Yes. May I help you?" He flipped the file closed and rocked back in his roller chair, glad to have Chrissy's situation resolved.

"My name is Collin Grace. Does that mean anything to you?"

Collin Grace? Ian frowned. The hair on the back of his neck prickled. "Should it?"

Slowly, he brought his chair back to an upright position, nerves alert in a way that made no sense. He received phone calls all the time. Why did the name Collin Grace evoke an eerie sensation?

"I hope so." Tension was as evident in the other man's voice as in his. After a heavy pause and an exhaled breath, the caller said, "You see, when I was a kid I had a brother, two in fact. One was named Ian."

Flashes of last night's dream kaleidoscoped through Ian's head. He blinked rapidly, trying to dispel the sudden disturbing burst of pictures.

"Why would that have anything to do with me?"

"Because I think you're my brother."

The quietly spoken words were like a scream inside Ian's head. This guy was either nuts or badly mistaken. He didn't have any brothers.

"Sorry, that's not possible." He started to hang up but something in the man's voice stopped him.

"Are you sure? My brothers and I were separated by foster care. Ian was only four. We have reason to believe he was adopted and moved from Oklahoma to Louisiana."

Ian's pulse rate started to kick up. Visions from the dream came at him with the speed of a black light until he grew dizzy.

Wouldn't he remember if he had a brother somewhere? Wouldn't he know if he'd been adopted?

But he couldn't shake the fact that something about the caller's information rang true.

It couldn't be. It couldn't.

Sweat popped out on his forehead. Fear, like a tidal wave, rolled over him. He had to get off the phone.

"Sorry to disappoint you, Mr. Grace, but you've got the wrong man. I'm an only child."

With an uncharacteristic abruptness, he slammed the phone down. His hand shook against the receiver.

Thrusting his face in his hands, he tried to make sense of what had just happened. One thing for certain, he was rattled. And the question was why?

He had no memory of a brother or of any other life outside of Louisiana.

"Collin Grace." He said the name aloud. And as soon as he did, something inside him snapped. He heard—no, he *felt*—a small boy screaming, "Collin, Collin!"

"Collin," he whispered.

As if his heart would rip right out of his chest, he felt the anguish of the dirty little boy being dragged from a room, calling that name over and over again.

Not just any little boy. A four-year-old version of himself.

"Oh, God, please help me. What's happening here?"

This couldn't be possible. It couldn't be. He was the beloved only child of Robert and Margot Carpenter. His parents would have told him if he was adopted. And since they didn't, he couldn't be.

Could he?

The day he and Gretchen visited Baton Rouge came back in a flood. She'd asked about his baby book, and he didn't recall ever seeing one. Or even a single photo of his infancy. His mother plastered the house with a thousand pictures of him, but none as a baby.

He'd never thought that strange until now.

His mother's careful wording came back to him then. She always said, "We waited so long to get you," or "When we got you, we were the happiest couple in the world." She'd never said, "When you were born."

Other clues, inconsequential until now, began to surface.

The fears that they would abandon him, the dream, the key chain.

At the last thought, he frowned. *The key chain?* What did that have to do with anything?

Hand trembling, he took the tiny fish from his pocket, laid it on the desk and stared at the dull pewter for the longest time.

Turning the ichthus over, he read the Old Testament promise. "I will never leave you nor forsake you."

All his life the verse had brought him comfort. He had assumed his parents had given him the key chain when he was in the hospital with meningitis. Now he wasn't so sure.

But what was the connection? Why had he thought of this today?

He concentrated so hard, searched so deep that a headache began to throb at his temples.

What if the caller was right? What if he wasn't the person he'd always thought himself to be?

And if he wasn't Ian Carpenter, who was he?

He longed to call his mother and ask, but he couldn't. He couldn't hurt her that way. If she'd wanted him to know she would have told him long ago. And with her heart problems, asking was out of the question.

The old fear rose up inside that his thoughts were disloyal. That he would displease his mother and lose her love.

Foolish notions. But he couldn't shake the awful feeling.

Gretchen stopped in the Isaiah House dayroom to chitchat with some of the residents she'd come to know. They seemed less intimidated by her presence these days, and she wasn't sure if that was a good or a bad thing. All of them knew that anything they said or did could easily end up on the six o'clock news, though her primary focus lately was the Riverside Shelter where rumors of inappropriate conduct between the director and the female residents ran amok.

The threat of an audit at Isaiah House paled in comparison to that. All charities went through them now and then.

She felt good today. Chipper. Happy.

Last night's long talk with Ian about the cult had been surprisingly freeing. Funny how getting the experience out in the light of day helped. Ian's gentle wisdom had given her hope that she could find answers. And maybe even make peace with God.

Maybe. She would take her slow, easy time to decide if Ian's God was any different from Brother Gordon's.

Gretchen patted a curly-haired teen on the shoulder and started up the narrow, wooden stairs.

Last night's date had been fun. Revealing, too. He liked her. The knowledge filled her with a kind of feminine power. She liked him, too. More than liked. That's why she'd been so disappointed when he hadn't kissed her good-night. So she'd kissed him.

A little thrill ran through her. Next time, she'd do a better job of it.

Smiling, she hummed all the way up the steps to his office. The door was closed and all was quiet inside. She tapped softly and stuck her head inside.

"Ian?"

He was sitting at his desk, staring into space.

Goodness, he was handsome.

Her pulse fluttered. For once, she didn't fight it.

"Hey, Reverend." She tapped on the door facing. "Anybody home?"

As if in a daze, Ian turned his head toward her, expression blank. Normally full of wit and welcome, he didn't say a word.

"Did I interrupt something?" Perhaps he'd been praying.

He let out a gusty breath and rubbed at his temples. "Why would you ask that?"

What an odd reply. "Is everything okay?"

"Fine. Did you need something?"

Need something? She blinked at him, confused.

He behaved as if they were strangers again, back to square one. Gretchen didn't like the feeling. Where was the guy from last night who'd held her hand and made her laugh and wanted to kiss her so badly, he'd stuck his hands in his pockets to keep them off her?

"Yeah, I do need something. Lunch. We discussed this last night. Remember? You invited me."

"Oh yeah. Sure." His gaze flickered to the telephone.

"My treat today. The weather's great. I'm in a good mood. All is right with the world. What do you say we walk down to Central Grocery and share a muffaletta?"

Her *joie de vivre* was lost on Ian.

"I'm pretty busy here."

"Well, okay. I can run down there, grab a sandwich and bring it back here. We can eat out on the balcony in the sunshine. I'll even let you play me a song or two. It'll be perfect."

"Look, Gretchen, I'd rather not. Okay?"

The terse comment hurt. "You're acting funny, Ian. What's wrong? Did I do something?"

Was he upset about the kiss on the cheek? Or had she revealed too much of herself to him last night? Did he, as she had feared, hold her past against her?

Crossing her arms, she stepped away and went to the French doors that opened onto the balcony. She'd come up here today full of hope and joy and excitement for the relationship developing between them. Now she was embarrassed.

Behind her, chair rollers clattered. Ian's tennis shoes made soft sounds as he came closer. She turned toward him, hoping he'd touch her. He didn't.

He stood apart, looking lost and anxious.

"You didn't do anything. I'm sorry." He rubbed at his shoulder muscle. "I've had a rough morning. That's all."

Ian never got much sleep, but he looked exhausted today. Worry cast fine lines around his eyes. And there was something else in those baby blues that she'd never witnessed before. Fear.

"Is there some kind of trouble here at the mission?" The audit wasn't even a done deal. It couldn't be that.

"You'd like that, wouldn't you?"

The accusation hurt. "No. I wouldn't."

Not now. Not when I've started to fall in love with you. Not when I have hope again. "I stopped hoping for the worst when we became—friends."

She choked out the final word, afraid she'd given her feelings away. The man wouldn't even kiss her. She had no right to assume anything about their relationship.

He relented then and took a step closer. "Forgive me, okay? I shouldn't have said that. This is no excuse for bad behavior, but I have a lousy headache."

"Is your mom okay?"

He jerked. "What?"

"Your mother. I thought maybe you'd gotten some bad news or something."

"I haven't called her yet. I guess I need to do that." His voice trailed away and he looked at the telephone again.

She wanted to ask if they were still on for the trip to Baton Rouge next week but decided this was not the time.

Dazed, troubled, worried. All those adjectives described Ian this morning.

As if he'd forgotten her presence, he walked out on the balcony and stood at the rail, staring down at the courtyard. She wanted to go to him, to put her arms around his waist and comfort him, though she had no idea why.

A horrible foreboding came over her. If there was trouble at the mission, she was the last person on earth he'd ever tell.

Silent and thoughtful, she watched him for a long time, dappled in sunlight with the soft, velvet breeze teasing his dark hair.

Something was amiss. Ian never behaved this way. He was a people person, warm, friendly and courteous to a fault. He would never intentionally ignore someone unless his own concerns were overwhelming.

Suspicion lifted its snakelike head. If Ian's problem lay here in the mission, finding out was her job.

The idea gave her no satisfaction whatsoever.

* * *

A week later, Ian, feeling like a jerk, was still avoiding Gretchen. Some of his initial shock after the bizarre phone conversation had dissipated, but he wasn't ready to be in line with Gretchen's radar.

She'd called at least a dozen times, left that many messages, but he hadn't returned the calls.

He owed her an explanation, but what could he say? "I may not be who you think I am, but I'm not sure."

If that wouldn't be like saying sic 'em to a Doberman, he didn't know what would. She already distrusted ministers. Here would be proof positive that he was another deceitful preacher, hiding behind God.

The whole idea that he might have an entire life he couldn't remember was insane even to him. She'd never believe it. Even a four-year-old had memories. But he had none. Zero. Zip. Nada. No knowledge of brothers or of being adopted.

And yet, he couldn't shake the feeling that he knew Collin Grace. That the man's claims had validity.

Somehow he had to discover the facts for himself, starting today during the trip to Baton Rouge.

Tying his newest pair of tennis shoes, he stuck the last two pair in a bag, determined to find new owners for them. Tabitha was more right than he wanted her to be. There was something psychological about his shoe purchases. He'd bought three new pair since that disturbing phone call.

He jogged downstairs, stopped at Roger's office for a quick discussion of next week's fund-raiser, and then headed to his van.

The back tire was flat.

He glanced at his watch. Eleven o'clock. Mom's appointment was at one-fifteen. He'd be cutting it close. Real close.

The old van was about worn-out. Next spring he'd think about buying another if finances allowed. He might even buy a real car for a change.

Yanking open the cargo door, he dug under the backseat for his jack. A car horn startled him. He jerked upright and bumped his head.

"Need a ride, stranger?" a feminine voice called.

Gretchen. His heart leaped. "Looks that way."

He couldn't be late today. His mother needed him, and he needed time in his boyhood home to dig through files and see what he could find.

Head smarting, he slammed the van door, locked it, then slid into Gretchen's sporty little Miata.

"You were going to stand me up, weren't you?" she said as soon as he buckled his seat belt.

Yes, he was. "I figured the date was off."

"Why? Because you've been avoiding me?"

"You're straightforward, aren't you?"

"A reporter who mealy-mouths around doesn't get far. I'm honest. I thought you of all people would return the favor." She gave him a look as she shifted into gear and pulled out into the flow of traffic. "Did I do something wrong?"

He adjusted his seat and turned toward her. Green eyes flashing, her stubborn chin jutted toward the highway. She wouldn't be easy on him today.

"No. You didn't." How did he explain? "I have a lot on my mind lately."

"I noticed. I also noticed that you haven't returned my phone calls and whenever I've come by the mission you've been mysteriously unavailable. Don't you realize how suspicious that appears? What are you hiding from me?"

"Nothing's going on with the ministry, Gretchen. You have my word."

"Okay, then. It must be personal. Are you sorry we went out on that date? Are you angry because I kissed you on the cheek? Are you trying to give me the royal kiss-off? Because if you are, say so. Don't avoid me."

Oh boy. The ride to Baton Rouge was going to be a long one.

Chapter Thirteen

Ian thought his head would explode.

The auditors were on their way.

Not that his books weren't in stellar order. They were. But right now, he had about all he could handle.

"Lord, you said you'd never put more on us than we could stand." He looked toward the ceiling. "Could I get a second opinion here?"

As had been the case for days, the prayer seemed to hit the stucco ceiling and bounce back.

Yesterday's trip to Baton Rouge had revealed nothing to answer his head full of questions. During the little time he'd had alone at Mom's house, he'd found no evidence of an adoption. But he hadn't found any baby pictures, either.

He had, however, learned a couple of things. Neither of them made him particularly happy.

His mother's heart was wearing out. And he was in love with Gretchen.

He'd never noticed before how much alike the two women were. Though of different styles, both were strong and bulldog determined. Neither had the word quit in her vocabulary. And both were imbued with an innate kindness. While Mom was a "bless-your-heart" Southerner, Gretchen was much more direct, but no less effective. Together they were a formidable force.

To his amusement and, if he'd admit it, his relief, the two woman had formed an iron front, peppering the doctors with questions and funny comments that kept everyone's spirits up during the trying round of tests.

When the diagnosis came down, Mom had waved the bad news away with one thin, aging hand. "I'll go when the Lord wants me and not a moment before."

Afterward, she'd refused to discuss her health further and had taken them all out to a Mexican restaurant and then to a movie.

Ian figured Gretchen had a better chance of getting his mother to comply with doctor's orders than he did.

"Gretchen." When the barracuda of Channel Eleven had pushed into his life, he'd expected trouble. He'd been more right than he could ever imagine.

The resident knot in his neck became a boulder.

Watching her hound the doctors and entertain him and his mother had stolen his heart forever. Part of him was ecstatic. But the other part knew the relationship had no future unless Gretchen found her way back to God. No matter how much he wanted to push the issue, faith was a private matter and an individual choice.

And even if she did, would she be interested in

him, a small-time street preacher who wasn't even sure who he was?

He blew out a weary breath. What little sleep he'd gotten last night had been filled with the dream. This time, he'd awakened in a sweat, screaming Collin's name.

Was he crazy? Had the years of sleeping little and working too much with troubled souls caused him to believe the bizarre tale that he wasn't Ian Carpenter? Or was he, as he feared, a total stranger to himself?

How could he ever expect Gretchen or anyone else to understand that his entire life had been a lie?

Until he could verify or disprove Collin's claim, he couldn't rest. But he had no idea how to do either without hurting his mother. He'd heard nothing more from Collin, but gut instinct said it was only a matter of time.

He pushed Roger's extension to let him know the auditors were here. Business at the mission couldn't wait while he sorted out his personal problems.

In three minutes flat, his bookkeeper burst into his office.

Hair wild as if he'd run his hands through it a dozen times, eyes wide, skin pastier than usual, Roger said, "Call them back. Make them wait. We can't start the audit today."

Bewildered, Ian asked, "Why not?"

"We just can't. Not yet. I need more time."

A cold fear snaked up Ian's spine. "More time for what? What are you not telling me?"

Roger collapsed into the only other chair in the room. His harsh breathing was the only sound for several seconds while Ian prayed that there was nothing wrong with the ministry's finances.

"I don't know how to tell you." Roger's long bony hands clenched and unclenched on his khaki-covered knees. "I failed you, Ian. I failed God. I didn't mean to. I was trying to do something right for once in my life, but I need more time to straighten everything out."

A trembling started way down deep in Ian's gut. Something was very, very wrong. "Tell me what's going on."

"I'm going to pay it back, Ian. I swear. It was a loan."

The trembling grew to quakes. Not Roger. Not his trusted friend.

"You took money from Isaiah House?" His voice was barely a whisper.

"A loan, Ian. You have to believe me." Roger raked shaky fingers through greasy hair, already awry. "I'd never steal from you. It was a loan."

Ian sank lower in his chair and prayed for wisdom and a calm he couldn't seem to find lately. Hands folded, he tapped thumb knuckles against his chin, desperately seeking the grace that had always carried him through.

Grace, Lord. Grace.

Yet, he couldn't even remember what grace meant at the moment.

His trusted friend sat before him about to confess to a crime that could ruin Isaiah House. There was no grace in such an admission.

"From the beginning. Spill it."

"I have a son."

Ian blinked. "You never told me."

"I figured he was better off without me. His mother

moved him out of state a long time ago." He rocked forward in the chair, intense, agitated. "You don't know what it's like, Ian, to be a father. I wasn't always a drunk. When Ronnie was little he tagged after me and wanted to be just like Daddy." His lips twisted bitterly. "He succeeded."

"What do you mean?"

"He's gotten into some trouble down in Mexico. If he's convicted, he'll be in prison for the rest of his life! You know what Mexican jails are like. I can't leave him there to rot."

"Drugs?" Ian guessed.

Roger nodded. A strand of greasy hair flopped forward. "You know what they do to drug smugglers down there."

He didn't, but he could guess.

"I've never done anything good for that kid. Just this once he needed me to be his father, and I couldn't turn my back. Not this time. Not when he cried to me over the telephone. He was scared, Ian. Scared and alone. We found a lawyer down there. With enough money to the right people, the lawyer can get him off. I had no choice."

"You're talking about bribes."

"I don't know. All I know for sure is that this lawyer says for enough money Ronnie can come home."

Incredulous, Ian asked, "And you thought taking from the ministry was the answer?"

"I knew you wouldn't understand. That's why I didn't tell you. You had a good father to learn from. My boy never did. It's my fault he ended up in trouble. How can

I claim to be a Christian and turn my back on my own son when he needed me most?"

"Do you realize how twisted that sounds, Roger? You stole from the ministry to do a Christian deed? That doesn't make sense."

"A loan, Ian." Roger's volume rose. "I'm telling you I borrowed the money."

"How did you plan to pay it back? And when?"

Roger slid lower in his chair, the hangdog expression filled with despair. "Ronnie's mother, my ex, has been trying to get a bank loan. No luck yet."

Stomach churning, Ian tapped the desktop. "How much money are we talking about?"

"Twenty thousand."

Ian's heart nearly stopped. "Twenty thousand! How? How did you do that without me noticing?"

"You don't pay much attention to the books."

Another failing on his part.

"What about the budget report each month to the board?"

He knew the answer as soon as he asked. The records were kept by hand. Roger could have altered the report without any of them noticing, especially in the area of cash donations.

He suspected now that Roger had taken the cash at Christmas, too, to divert attention elsewhere in case he checked the accounts at year's end. Like a fool, he hadn't.

Disappointment mixed with bitter realization settled over Ian like a depression. His friend had been afraid to ask him for help.

"You should have told me. I would have helped."

The harried man rose and paced to the French doors, then turned and paced back, spreading his hands in a pleading gesture. "Then, help me now. He's my son. And I've got a record."

"I know."

"They'll send me to prison."

"I won't let that happen." Though he had no clue what to do to stop it. "Let me call our attorney, talk this over with him."

"No! I'm responsible. I'll face the consequences head-on. All I ask is that you let me get my son out of Mexico first. Please, Ian, friend to friend. If the press gets wind of this, Ronnie will be stuck in a foreign prison for the rest of his life. Keep my name clear until he's safely across the border."

The pounding in Ian's temples grew exponentially. His sympathy for his friend wrestled with ethics. What was the right thing to do? Betray a friend, and his son, for the sake of the mission's reputation? Or help a friend in need and hope for the best?

The hammering in his brain accused him. If he'd been the minister and friend he claimed to be, Roger would have come to him first.

"How much time do you need?" He couldn't believe he was actually considering this. And the scary part was he didn't know if it was right or wrong.

"I'm not sure. I wired the money more than a week ago, but the wheels don't turn as fast down there as they do here."

"The audit will take a few days, maybe longer. Maybe we've got time."

* * *

Gretchen snapped her briefcase shut and extended her hand. "Thanks for your cooperation, Reverend Connely. I think we have everything we need."

The final segment on Second Chance Ministries would air tonight. Unlike Riverside Shelter, this report would spotlight a well-run drug-recovery ministry that citizens could support without reservation.

"Your cell's ringing." Jonathon, her photographer, motioned toward the van. She loped over to answer it, hoping to find Ian on the other end. During yesterday's trip to Baton Rouge, they'd regained some sense of camaraderie, although he'd seemed unusually preoccupied. But what did she expect? He was overworked at the mission and now his mother was ill.

Five minutes later, she squinted up at the bright sky and wished she'd gone into some other occupation. The auditors at Isaiah House, according to her tipsters, had found a serious discrepancy. And Ian refused to discuss it.

A few months ago, she would have danced around the van in victory at any allegations against Isaiah House. In her eagerness to blame Ian for Maddy's death, she'd focused far too much attention on the mission for runaways.

A sick feeling burned her throat. She didn't want Ian to be dirty. She loved him. All her instincts, however, had been warning her for days that something was very wrong in Ian's world.

"Trouble?" Jonathon said as he loaded camera and gear into the back of the Channel Eleven SUV.

"I hope not." She shoved her briefcase behind the

seat and slammed the door. "Drop me off at Isaiah House."

"Don't you need a photographer?"

"No. I only need some answers."

She didn't get them.

What she did get was more to worry about.

From outward appearances Isaiah House was the same as always. After greeting a handful of kids coming out of a meeting room, she started upstairs to Ian's office.

She heard his quiet voice long before she made the top step. His door was open. He stood at the French doors looking out, a cordless telephone against his ear. Something in his stance made her pause.

"Yes. I have it." The tension in his words raised prickles on her skin. Something was going on here. As a friend she wanted to make her presence known. As a reporter, she needed to listen unobserved.

Quietly, she backed out and waited in the hall out of sight.

"I'd rather no one else know about this. I need a little more time."

Silence.

And then, "Treehouse Restaurant? In the atrium. Sure, I know the place. Seven o'clock is as good a time as any, I guess." He sounded strained, nervous, maybe even scared. "I'll bring it with me."

The Treehouse was about as far away from the French Quarter as he could get and still be in New Orleans. No one would recognize him there.

Gretchen's investigative antenna went on red alert.

Whatever was going on must be connected with the allegations of embezzled ministry funds. But what could it be? She was certain he wasn't involved with drugs. Gambling, perhaps? Was that it? Was he over his head in gambling debt? Or maybe blackmail for some indiscretion?

Somehow she couldn't reconcile the Ian she knew with a man who would take money from his own ministry. Yes, she knew it happened all the time, but not Ian. Not the man she loved.

Dismay as heavy as a monster truck pressed down on her. For months, she'd dug for this kind of shady story, but instead of feeling victorious she was heartbroken.

She'd wanted Ian to be what he seemed to be. To think that he might be a wolf in sheep's clothing hurt too much. There had to be a mistake. Surely, she wasn't such a fool that she would fall in love with a charlatan after all she'd been through with the Family of Love.

Standing in the hallway, she gathered her scattered thoughts and screaming emotions into hand. Following a few minutes of silence in the office, music from a saxophone began to play.

Gretchen put her face in her hands. She loved hearing him play. Though she didn't recognize the melody, she recognized the emotion. Ian was hurting.

Everything in her screamed to go to him, to comfort him, but she couldn't. She wouldn't. Not until she knew for sure that he was exactly who and what he claimed to be.

When the music trembled into silence, Gretchen forced a happy face and knocked on the doorjamb.

Ian, his back still to the doorway, turned, saxophone tilted against one shoulder. "Gretchen. Hey."

He didn't smile.

"Got a minute?" He looked so tired.

"Sure. Come in."

"The music was sad. You okay?"

"Yeah." He set the saxophone into a stand against the wall and straightened, turning toward her. "No, I'm not. Not really."

"I knew that. Want to talk about it?"

For once he didn't ask if she was on the record or off. She was relieved because as much as she despised the situation, anything he said was on the record.

"Want a soda?" he asked, going to the tiny fridge behind his desk.

"Sounds good." Watching him, trying to gauge what was happening behind those beautiful blue eyes, Gretchen settled into a chair.

He took two orange sodas, popped the tops and handed one to her. He leaned against the front of his desk, tennis shoes angled out in front of him. Another new pair, she noticed. Surely, a man wouldn't embezzle money to buy tennis shoes.

Instead of sipping his drink, Ian fiddled with the can's tab. His mind seemed to be preoccupied and distant.

When he spoke, she had the feeling that he barely knew she was there.

"Have you ever had to do something, that you're not sure if it's right or wrong?"

Did he mean like now when she was pumping him for information and all she really wanted was to throw her arms around him and promise that everything would be all right?

"Have you?"

"Something's going on here, Gretchen. Several things actually. I wish I could share the facts with you."

"But you can't?"

"No."

The admission hurt. "Because of my job?"

He pointed a finger at her, a half smile lifting his lips. "Bingo."

"I know about the problems with the audit."

He flinched. "Is this going on television?"

"Are you guilty?" Please say no.

"I'd rather not talk about that right now."

Which meant he probably was. The heaviness in her chest pushed upward until she thought her throat would swell closed.

"I need you to be honest with me, Ian."

"For the report or for yourself?"

"Both." Her hand grew slick on the cold soda can. "I care about you." Boy, was that a gross understatement.

His eyes studied her with a sadness that was wrenching. "I know you do."

She waited, hoping to hear him admit he cared, too. He didn't.

Had she misunderstood the signals? Was she so messed up that she didn't know when a man was falling in love with her?

Angry at herself, Gretchen jerked upright. "You're not going to tell me anything, are you?"

"I wish I could."

"You said that already." She slapped the soda onto his desk. Orange liquid splashed out. He hadn't mentioned the phone call and now he refused to discuss the financial discrepancies. A man who wouldn't talk usually had something to hide.

And knowing that was killing her.

She loved him, for crying out loud!

With effort, she said, "Look, you've had a rough day. Why don't we forget all this for a while and go somewhere for a nice dinner? I'll make you laugh and forget your troubles." She held up two fingers. "Promise. I should be finished at the station by six. We could meet somewhere at say, seven?"

Backing him into a corner was a sneaky thing to do. But she had to give him one more chance to tell her where he was going tonight.

Ian rolled the pop can back and forth between his palms. "Could I take a rain check?"

"You're too busy to eat?"

"You know my schedule. The soup kitchen, chapel, street patrol."

Not a word about his mysterious meeting.

All right, then. Fine. She stifled an inward sigh.

She'd find out for herself what he was hiding. And if Ian Carpenter had a dirty secret, she'd have no choice but to tell the world.

Chapter Fourteen

Holding the flip phone to her ear, Gretchen pulled her Mazda to a stop at a red light. Rush hour traffic bunched up around her as if the Miata was magnetized. One jerk was so close she could practically smell his breath.

Some days she wanted to live in the swamps.

To add to an already tense afternoon, her hyperactive boss had called three times. "I've heard rumblings. What do you have on the Isaiah House audit?"

She glanced in the rearview mirror at the idiot riding her bumper. If the guy knew how stressed she was, he'd back off. Road rage was becoming more understandable by the minute.

"The Second Chances report goes on tonight, not Isaiah House."

"Your favorite councilwoman has sources who claim there is a problem with the audit out there. We need that story."

Gretchen tensed. Right now, her heart was breaking, her mind was racing, and the last thing she needed was Marian Jacobs interfering with the way she did her job.

"The report is still developing, Mike. I won't go live without facts."

"Then get some. We don't need a popular politician breathing down our necks."

"When did Marian Jacobs start running the newsroom?"

Mike was silent for so long Gretchen wished she'd kept her mouth shut. When he spoke, the words were terse and to the point.

"Get me a story. Tonight."

"I can't."

"You're an investigative reporter. A good one. Don't let a preacher's pretty face keep you from doing a good job, Gretchen. The public depends on your integrity."

The man didn't play fair. He'd gone straight for her most vulnerable spot. People did have a right to know if something was wrong at Isaiah House. Not only were donations at issue, but kids' lives, as well.

"All right then. I'll do what I can." The light changed and the car behind her honked before she could even get her foot off the brake. Grinding her teeth, she accelerated. With one eye on the road, one on her rearview mirror and her ear to the phone, she was about as safe as a turtle on a freeway. She looked for a place to pull off but in this traffic she was stuck.

"How about a strong teaser to run at the end of tonight's segment?" she said.

Hopefully, after Ian's secret meeting, she'd have a teaser to send.

"That'll work. Make it good."

"You got it."

Flipping her phone shut, she gunned the Mazda to escape the guy who thought he was Dale Jr., then headed through the narrow streets and across Lake Pontchartrain toward the Treehouse Restaurant.

Promising a strong teaser was easy. Following through could be a little tricky.

The Treehouse was a cozy little place nestled amidst moss-laden oaks and weeping willows. Taking advantage of its name and surroundings, the Treehouse was a two-story structure with an atrium on the first floor. The result was a restaurant whose interior felt like an exterior. Plants, trees, bushes filled the place.

She asked for a table on the second floor and strategically maneuvered to be seated overlooking the atrium. The establishment was moderately busy though Ian had yet to arrive. She searched the faces wondering which person waited for him. And why.

No one looked the least bit suspicious. Voices drifted upward along with delightful smells, but conversations were indistinct.

Not good. She could see and smell, but not hear.

As she was debating a seat change, Ian entered the atrium. Her heart fluttered foolishly. He looked so handsome wearing a sport jacket over a blue shirt. A waitress attired in camouflage shorts and camp shirt showed him to a table where a tall, muscular man sat alone. He stood to greet Ian. Neither of them smiled.

From this distance, a cell phone video was basically worthless. Taking her digital camera, she snapped a photo as the two exchanged tense, polite handshakes.

Something serious was going on all right.

Ian spoke to the waitress and then folded his hands on the tabletop. Though his back was to her, his posture screamed anxiety.

The dark stranger began to talk, but Gretchen could make out nothing. It drove her crazy not to know what was being said. She considered going downstairs, but Ian would see her. There was nothing to do but watch and wait. Later, when she confronted Ian with her evidence, he would have no choice but to explain or lie. She hoped he cared for her enough to tell the truth. Either way, she'd have a teaser.

Not caring one whit about food, she picked the first thing on the menu and quickly placed her order. With the churning in her stomach, she might be sick at any moment.

Eyes glued to the tense scene below, she watched Ian lay something on the table. She strained forward trying to see but couldn't make out the object. What in the world could it be?

The stranger shifted forward and flipped open his jacket.

Gretchen gasped. Breath froze in her throat.

Snugged close to the man's side was a shoulder holster, complete with revolver.

She snapped a picture.

Ian was in much deeper trouble than she'd ever dreamed.

"Oh, Ian," she whispered. "What have you done?"

For once, she was waist deep in a situation that all her inner strength and self-reliance couldn't handle. Her job demanded that she follow the story to its end and report the truth, even if Ian was a criminal.

Her heart cried to protect the man she loved.

She squeezed her eyes closed. She didn't know if God would help, but Ian was worth the effort.

Ian stared down at the two identical fish key chains as his world crashed in around him. Collin Grace was painfully familiar. And something deep inside Ian responded to the story he told of a childhood Ian couldn't fully remember but that sounded frighteningly like the nightmare that haunted him.

He rubbed a hand across his eyes. Was this man his brother?

Collin seemed like a good guy. A SWAT cop, he'd said, from Oklahoma City. A Christian, too. He even gave God the credit for discovering Ian's whereabouts.

Collin tapped the ichthus. "All three of us were given one of these by the counselor the day we were separated."

"My parents gave me this key chain when I was in the hospital."

Collin's cop eyes, much darker than his own blue ones, narrowed. "Are you sure?"

He wasn't. He'd never really known where the little token had come from and for some reason he'd never been comfortable enough to ask.

His silence must have been telling because Collin didn't press. Instead he said, "Why were you in the hospital?"

"Meningitis. When I was five."

"You remember that? The hospital and all?"

"Sort of. I was pretty sick. But my mother—" He stumbled over the word. *Was* she his mother? "Mom has pictures."

The waitress brought iced tea. Glad for the interruption, Ian took a sip to clear his dry throat. "Anyone could have a key chain like this. They aren't exactly rare."

Collin shook his head. The dark military-style haircut befitting a SWAT cop glistened beneath the restaurant's bright lights. "Not rare, but old. I haven't seen another one like it in a long time. But I have other more conclusive evidence."

Once again Collin reached inside his jacket. This time he withdrew an envelope. "From the welfare office. Bits about the adoption."

The word adoption screamed at him. Could his entire life have been nothing but an illusion created by adoptive parents? "Bits?"

"I can't get the originals." He didn't look at all happy about that. "Neither can you. The records are sealed. That's why I've had such a hard time tracking you down."

"None of this makes sense to me. I was old enough to remember something, so why don't I? And why would my parents lie to me? Why would they be so determined to hide the truth that they sealed the records?"

Another of Collin's long thoughtful pauses hung in the air between them. "Did you have a good life, Ian? Were your parents good to you?"

He thought of his happy childhood, of the two people

who had adored him and filled him with confidence and love. That didn't excuse the startling secret they'd kept from him. But that wasn't what Collin needed to hear and Ian wanted to ease the worry he saw in the man's face.

"Yes. They were terrific parents."

A little of the tension seeped out of Collin's broad shoulders. "During the time I was in foster care, I searched for you, and all the years since. I never stopped hoping that you and Drew had been adopted together. That you'd found a family. I wanted that for you."

The unspoken pain was there. Collin had grown up in the social system, a lousy place for a kid, though he appeared to have done all right. Apparently the other sibling, Drew, hadn't found a family, either.

"Have you found Drew?"

A shadow of sorrow slid over Collin's serious face. "Let's discuss that later, okay? After I've convinced you that we're brothers."

Either Drew hadn't been found or something bad had happened to him. From Ian's work with runaways, he knew the end result for many troubled kids, especially those lost in the system. Drugs, gangs, crime, lives of desperate dysfunction. He shuddered to think that he might have been one of those statistics.

His gaze dropped to the table.

The copied paper looked like rattlesnakes. He didn't want to look, and yet he was fascinated. Was his true identity folded inside these few sheets?

Slowly, he unfolded the documents. A worn, curled photo of three little boys looked out at him. His stomach went south. He recognized those faces. They haunted his dreams.

He swallowed hard. The document in his hands trembled. As some deep, inner glimmering stirred, Ian glanced up at the dark, intense man.

"It's you, Ian. And me. And Drew. I took care of you when you were small. Don't you think I'd recognize you?"

Heart keeping a jungle rhythm against his rib cage, Ian muttered, "We were so young."

Then he stopped, not ready to admit that his mother had lied to him for years and that he was not at all who he believed himself to be. Yet the evidence lay before him.

And, of course, there was Collin. Something inside him yearned toward this man. He'd always wanted a brother.

"If we're brothers, why don't I remember?"

"That's the puzzle. I don't know. The meningitis maybe?"

"Is that possible?"

The side of Collin's mouth lifted. "Lately, I'm finding that all things are possible. I've looked for you all my life and now here you are."

Sweat beaded under Ian's collar. He slid the documents along with the photo back into the manila envelope. "How long?"

"Every single day of every single week. Since the day the social worker dragged you kicking and screaming out of her office."

Chills raced up his back. The dream pushed at his mind. Was the nightmare a reality? A repressed memory he'd lived through? Was that why he could never escape it?

He took a breath, tried to get hold of the trembling inside. "Start at the beginning. Tell me what happened."

Collin studied him for a few seconds, the intense brown eyes weighing what to say and how to say it. His desire to find his long-lost brothers was a palpable thing. Ian didn't want to disappoint him, and yet the alternative scared him to pieces.

What kind of man would spend his entire life searching for lost siblings? The answer was clear. A man of deep commitment and responsibility who loved his little brothers. The idea made listening a lot easier. If he had to choose a brother, Collin Grace would be a good one.

"The story's ugly," Collin said. "Common, but still ugly." He stirred a spoon of sugar into his tea but didn't drink. "Our birth mother was a crack addict. I don't remember when she started. After your dad left I think. I'm not sure. I'm not even sure if he was my dad, too, or only yours. All I remember is that Mama was gone a lot. Sometimes for days. We spent enough time in foster care for me to know that wasn't the life I wanted for any of us. But that's what happened."

Collin went on, telling tales of living in rat-infested houses and old cars. Of going hungry and being scared. But he also told of three brothers whose bond of love had kept them together and fighting for life until welfare stepped in.

Collin spread wide hands on the table. "I tried, Ian. I tried to take care of you and Drew. I tried to keep us together like I promised."

"You were a kid, too."

"I was the oldest. You were my responsibility, my

brothers, my best friends. All we had was each other. You needed me." His voice dropped, low and intense. "I needed you, too."

Some vagary, just out of reach, scraped at the edges of Ian's memory. He fiddled with the tiny pewter fish trying to remember something, anything before the time in the hospital. "The day we were separated. That last day..."

"I'll never forget it. The social worker took us to her office from the school. It was cold outside. I knew—" he tapped his chest with one finger "—I knew what was going to happen but couldn't do a thing to stop it. You were wearing a plaid flannel shirt and shoes without strings. Little and skinny and unaware that the world was coming to an end. A social worker took you by the hand and started the car, leaving me and Drew behind at the welfare office. When you realized what was happening you started to scream." Collin squeezed his eyes shut. When he opened them, his voice grew soft. "I can still hear you screaming my name."

Collin. Collin. Collin!

Ian heard it, too, deep inside his soul.

And then he knew. As if floodgates had opened, memories tumbled in, one on top of the other, so fast Ian feared he couldn't contain them all.

His heart pounded so radically, he wondered if he'd have a heart attack.

Collin. His big brave brother. The boy in the dream who comforted him when he cried.

Love mixed with sorrow slammed through him.

"You taught me to tie my shoes," he murmured through

a mouth dry as cotton. "I was sitting in the sun. In the backyard on something metal."

Collin leaned forward, face intense. "An old car hood. Blue and rust."

Ian lifted eyes full of knowledge to stare into the face of his beloved brother. "You stole food for us."

His brother's jaw tightened. "When I had to."

Little boy though he'd been, Collin had served as a surrogate parent to him and Drew. He'd done things no child should have to do. Lied, stolen, found shelter and food and clothes for his little brothers.

"You always said you weren't hungry. But you were." Tears welled in Ian's eyes. "I didn't understand that then. I was so little…"

He felt guilty for all the times he'd eaten Collin's share.

Collin hitched a shoulder as though denying himself food so that Ian and Drew could eat was no big deal.

Overwhelmed with emotion, Ian couldn't talk. He couldn't think. His chest ached. He was a grown man and he wanted to fall into Collin's arms like a little kid and cry. The way he'd done when he was four-years-old.

Collin must have seen the truth in his face. He reached out, gripped the top of Ian's hand and said, "You all right?"

"I need some time, okay?" Ian choked out. Time to pray, time to figure out why he'd never remembered before and why his mother hadn't told him.

He shoved back from the table, insides trembling with raw emotion. Collin rose, too, quiet, intense, and waiting.

"I'm at the Sheraton. Give me a call when you're ready."

Head thundering with images, mind whirling with the revelation, stunned and dazed, Ian turned to leave and then twisted back to the man who had just torn his world apart while putting it back together. "Collin."

"Yeah?"

"I'll call. I promise."

For the first time, the big, intense man's face softened, and he smiled.

Chapter Fifteen

Gretchen ground her teeth in frustration as she maneuvered through traffic. Why didn't these people stay home?

By the time she'd paid for the fettuccine she hadn't eaten and rushed out into the parking lot, both Ian and the stranger had disappeared.

She slammed the heel of her hand against the steering wheel. The clock on the dash glowed the time in bright yellow. Mike expected a teaser before the last broadcast. And all she had was innuendo and some fuzzy photos.

To make things worse, she had no desire to do her job. She wanted to talk to Ian, find out what was happening. More than that, she wanted him to share whatever was bothering him lately. After tonight, she suspected the worst, but she could handle it. What she couldn't handle was losing him.

The truth hit her like a brick through the windshield.

Ian's opinion of her had become more important than anything else in her life. She was in danger of falling into the religion trap again, fooled by a smooth, sweet-talking preacher. She couldn't let that happen.

"Not again. Never again."

And yet the very heart of her cried out against betraying Ian. She had the power to destroy Isaiah House, to make sure that no sensible human ever donated to the mission again. Was that the right thing to do? Did Ian deserve that? Even if he'd made some kind of mistake, didn't he deserve a second chance? She knew him too well now to believe he would take funds from the mission without a very good reason. But was any reason good enough when the best interest of the public was in question?

Ian was the only one who knew the answers.

Instead of going to the television station as she'd planned, Gretchen, mind spinning, headed toward Isaiah House. If Ian was the man she wanted him to be, he'd be man enough to answer all her questions. And if he didn't, the refusal would be a different kind of answer altogether. Either way, she'd know.

So she didn't lose her nerve, she phoned her boss to renew the promise. She'd be back at the station in time to film that teaser, whether positive or negative. The choice was up to Ian.

She hurried into the mission and raced up the steps to Ian's office. He wasn't there.

Frustration mounting, she started back down, passed his private quarters. On a hunch, she pounded on the door.

Several long seconds passed while she tapped her foot impatiently on the hardwood flooring. "Are you in there?"

The lock clicked and the door swung open. She stormed inside. "You lied."

"Nice to see you, too."

"Don't try your sweet talk on me. It won't work anymore. I need answers and I need them now." She paced to a chair, grabbed a pillow and threw it at the bed.

Ian's frown moved from her face to the tossed pillow and back again. "What are you talking about?"

She couldn't help noticing the strain around his mouth and the worry in his electric-blue eyes. Even annoyed, she loved his eyes.

"I saw you at the Treehouse."

A beat passed and then, "Since when do I have to tell you about my dinner plans?"

That hurt. "You led me to believe you were having a routine evening."

"But you followed me anyway." Ian's nostrils flared, then his shoulders slumped as if his strength was gone. "I should probably be angry about that but…"

"I knew something was wrong."

"Nothing's wrong."

"Another lie." She stopped pacing the small room and glared at him. "That man had a gun."

"That man—" Hands on hips, he took a deep breath and blew it out. "Can we talk about this calmly? Please? I've had kind of a rough day."

His weariness was almost palpable. Whatever was wrong was taking a toll. As much as she wanted to be angry at his secretiveness, he was still Ian and she was worried about him.

"I thought we cared about each other, Ian. I thought we were at least friends." Did that sound pitiful or what? "Tell me what's going on."

"Sit down, okay? I'm afraid you're going to destroy my apartment." The hint of a grin softened the words.

The apartment as he called it wasn't much. The small space reminded her of a hotel room with a bed and nightstand, a television on a chest, and a small table and chairs jammed into the corner.

She chose one of the chairs. "Who was that man and why did you lie about meeting him?"

He held up a hand. "I didn't lie. I just didn't tell you."

She waved him off. "Whatever. Who was he? Why did he have a gun?"

"He's a cop."

Alarm raced up her spine. The problem with the audit must be worse than rumored. "Are you in big trouble?"

He smiled. The man was hub deep in hot water and he smiled. "No. At least, not the kind you're talking about. The meeting was personal business that has nothing to do with the mission."

Personal business. That could mean about anything, including something very illegal. "Are you going to tell me?"

After a long pause in which she'd imagined all sorts of nefarious activities, Ian said, "I have to make a trip to Baton Rouge and talk to my mother first. I can't risk having her upset by secondhand information."

A warning raised the hairs on her neck. If he was concerned about his mother finding out, the situation must be worse than she imagined. "Ian, what have you done?"

"Nothing worthy of your news channel. This is personal."

"Then let me help. I have a little savings if it's money you need."

He gave her a funny look. "Why do you think I need money?"

"That man at the restaurant. The gun. I saw you exchange something. Some papers and something else. You have to admit that's pretty suspicious."

Ian stared at her for two beats. "You're not going to let up, are you?"

"I can't."

He circled the room once, twice. Gretchen waited, silent and watchful. Ian was stressed like she'd never seen before.

Finally, he came to a stop in front of her. "His name is Collin Grace. He's my brother."

Her heart sank. He was lying. "You're an only child."

"So I thought." He scrubbed the heel of his hand over his forehead. "I was pretty shocked, let me tell you. Right now, I haven't absorbed all of it. I came back here to think and pray."

She wasn't buying any of this. If he thought he could make up some wild story to distract her from doing the report, he was crazy. And she was disappointed that he'd even try.

"How could he possibly be your brother?"

"Apparently I was adopted when I was four or five."

He was either too distraught to concoct a sensible lie

or he thought she was stupid. "At that age you would remember having a brother."

"That's the part that has me so bewildered." He sat down on the bed and put his head in his hands. "Give me a little time to think about it, okay? I have to talk to Mom first. For some reason, she's kept the truth from me. I have to know why."

Unless he was a great actor, he truly was upset and confused. The question remained, was the man his brother? And if so, was Ian distraught over the news or over something to do with the audit? Or were they one and the same? Was the brother a bad egg causing problems for his minister brother? Would Ian pay him off to keep him quiet?

"Is he blackmailing you?"

"What?"

"My sources say there's money missing in the audit."

His shoulders slumped. "Okay, then. Since you know that much, I'll admit it. But the money has nothing to do with Collin."

"You're telling me the two incidents, coming one on top of the other, are not related?"

"Yes, I am. And I'd rather you didn't mention either one for a few days."

He had to be kidding. "Ian, there's money missing from your accounts. I can't let that go."

"Give me a few days. That's all I'm asking."

"How much money are we talking about?" And what does it have to do with the man at the restaurant?

"Twenty thousand."

She struggled to keep calm. Did he not realize what a huge sum that was? "Who's responsible?"

With a kind of intensity she'd never seen in him, Ian paced to the table, picked up a Bible and flipped aimlessly through the pages before closing it again.

Finally, he looked at her and in the quietest possible voice said, "I am."

Her heart fell to her toes. "Oh, Ian. Why? Why?"

Eyes burning with the need to cry, she squeezed them shut. Her heart hurt with the knowledge that she'd done it again. Ian was no different from Brother Gordon.

A rustle of movement and Ian went down on his knees in front of her, taking her hands in his. His touch was warm and strong and sure. She should pull away but she couldn't.

"I didn't say I took the money. I said I'm responsible. Everything that happens here is my responsibility."

She wanted to believe him, but experience made her skeptical. "Are you covering for someone?"

And what did the man at the restaurant have to do with any of this?

He shook his head. "Isaiah House is a clean operation, Gretchen. We have our problems like any other place." He gave a mirthless laugh. "A lot of them lately, but the work we do has never suffered. You've been here. You've seen the changed lives."

He released her then and stood.

"All I'm asking is that you give me a little more time. Then I'll tell you everything."

"Give me a reason to believe you, Ian. You know I want to. Tell me what's going on."

"I wish I could." He spread his arms out to the side, vulnerable. "You know me. You know what kind of man I am. Sometimes you have to take things on blind faith."

"I don't know if I can."

"All right then. Forget me. This ministry has never been about me anyway. It's about Him. About doing the work that Jesus did. I don't care how I look in the press, but this house going under hurts the people who need help the most." Fist clenched, he stared up at the ceiling and then back at her. "It's about God, Gretchen, not about you or some news story. And it's sure not about me. It's about Him."

She couldn't understand what any of that had to do with the fact that someone had stolen a lot of money from the trusting donors.

"I have a job to do. I've made commitments."

"To your station?"

"To the public. To tell the truth."

"Whose truth? Yours? Mine? God's? When Channel Eleven aired the first negative report on Isaiah House, donations fell drastically. Kids in jeopardy were affected. Our work here for the needy has been affected. If this house goes down people suffer. *That's* truth."

"So was the story we aired."

"There we are, then. An impasse, because we both think we're right and neither is willing to budge."

"You could tell me what's going on. All of it, including the whole story about that man."

"I will."

"When?"

"As soon as I can."

Annoyance zipped through her. "Why are you doing this? I thought you cared about me."

"I do care, Gretchen."

"But you don't trust me."

When he didn't answer, she laughed, a bitter, pained sound. "You think I should trust you even though trouble is swirling around you like a cyclone, but you won't give me the same courtesy." She shot up out of the chair and stormed to the door.

"Where are you going?"

"I think you know."

"Don't do this, Gretchen. Give me a few days. A few hours. Some time. Don't. Please. You're going to hurt a lot of people."

One hand on the doorknob, she paused long enough to say, "You know what's really sad, Ian?" She let a beat pass until certain she had his full attention. "I'm in love with you."

As soon as her words registered on his face, she slammed the door and ran.

Ian started to follow and then changed his mind. Pursuit was futile. There was nothing else he could say or do to keep Isaiah House out of the news. He only prayed that this was not the beginning of the end for his life's work.

Back to the wall, he leaned his head against the cool plaster and closed his eyes. What a day. He'd made a mess of every single thing he'd done. From Roger to Collin to Gretchen.

He felt as if he'd swallowed a hot brick that now lodged in his chest.

Gretchen was in love with him.

Collin was his brother.

Roger's son was still in Mexico. And the auditors were closing in.

Head spinning with information overload, he didn't know what to worry about first. His work, his newfound brother, his mom, or the woman who spoke of love but wanted to ruin him. Nice paradox. Yet, why should he be surprised? His entire life had been a lie and he hadn't even known it.

He raised his eyes toward the ceiling. "You're the only thing left, Lord, that's not in a mess."

Deep inside, he questioned whether he should ever have agreed to Roger's request.

Not much he could do about it now.

Maybe he should have told Gretchen everything, but she'd been skeptical about Collin. She probably wouldn't believe anything he said tonight.

Gretchen was compassionate. She might understand.

The mission was at stake.

Indecision warred inside him.

"Lord, I don't know what to do." Could he trust an investigative newswoman to keep Roger's name clear until his son stepped foot on American soil?

He'd given his word to Roger.

Defeated, he put on his tennis shoes and ball cap in preparation for the night's work. Regardless of his own personal issues, the kids on the streets still needed him.

He headed for his van and the dark side of town.

* * *

Gretchen stumbled down the staircase, cheeks burning while her heart broke.

Why had she thrown her love in his face that way? He'd done nothing to deserve that.

Sometimes she didn't understand her own propensity for hurting other people.

At the bottom step, she heard the television in the dayroom and decided to go out the back way. She couldn't face any of the residents tonight. Not when they would all be out on the streets again after the news came out that Isaiah House was dirty.

Out on the streets again.

The words rang inside her head like a gong. She was tossing kids to the lions.

But she had a commitment to air the truth about ministries, no matter what.

The need to scream in frustration pushed at her throat. What was the right thing to do? Trust Ian? Save the mission and lose her job? Believe his off-the-wall story about having a long-lost brother?

Her huff of agitation rang in the quiet hallway. Confusion and trouble was what she got for falling in love with a preacher.

She paused in the hallway outside the chapel and stared at the framed poster proclaiming Matthew 25, the sister verse to Isaiah 58. Ian claimed these as his life verses. Feeding the hungry, caring for the sick, the broken, the stranger. Meeting the needs of the unlovely.

The final words of Christ on the poster convicted her.

"I tell you the truth, whatever you did for one of the least of these brothers of mine, you did for me."

True and undefiled religion. Unselfish. Giving. Even at the sacrifice of personal gain.

Stung, she tried to make sense of everything. This kind of personal sacrifice was Ian's life. She knew from watching him, from working with him that this was true. And it didn't mesh with reports of misappropriation or embezzlement. She'd known that all along.

Yet, she'd refused to believe the depth of Ian's commitment, not because of anything he did or didn't do, but because she had lost her faith in God.

A sob surprised her, rising up from somewhere deep inside as if it had been waiting for her eyes to open. She'd never been so confused.

Fist to her lips, she shoved into the chapel and stumbled into one of the padded seats. The room was empty and quiet except for her and a gentle, wooing presence. The glow of white sconces along the wall and around the cross added to the sense of peace.

Peace. She didn't even know what that was.

She sat quietly for a few minutes, thinking, soaking up the ambience of the holy little chapel, eyes fixed on the simple wooden cross in back of the platform.

"I don't know what to do, God. Are You here? Do You care? Have I been gone too long for You to hear me?"

Not since the days in the commune had she been willing to surrender control long enough to listen, to feel God's presence. She'd been too afraid that he would ask the unthinkable.

As soon as the thought arrived, Gretchen faced a

truth long denied. God had never asked the unthinkable of her. Man had. Ian had tried to tell her that, but now she understood. The selfish, greed for power of a human had hurt her and Maddy. Her family had blindly, foolishly followed Brother Gordon without question. How could she blame God for that?

"I'm sorry, Lord. I'm sorry."

The hard, hurting place inside began to ease. Quietly, she poured out all her hurts and fears in the dimly lit chapel.

No bells rang. No angels sang. The heavens didn't open. But the heavy load of care and guilt and shame lightened until her tears became a watery smile.

Digging in her pocket, she came up with a tissue and dabbed at her face. She had no idea how long she'd been in here. A few minutes? An hour?

She glanced at her watch. Ten minutes until the teaser was due.

A new resolve settled over her as sweet as the newfound peace.

The situation with Ian hadn't changed. The suggestion of wrongdoing was still present. But now she understood what she hadn't. Ian's actions in this mission were worthy of trust. Regardless of rumors or innuendos by disgruntled politicians and nearby businesses that wanted the troubled kids of Isaiah House moved elsewhere, Ian's work, day after day, spoke for itself.

Yes, something was very wrong here. Ian admitted as much. But Ian would take care of it in his own time and in an honorable manner. She believed that now.

A giggle bubbled in her throat.

Was she losing her mind?

The credibility of her career was about to be jeopardized.

And she wanted to laugh and sing for joy.

Chapter Sixteen

At five in the morning Ian showered and then grabbed a giant travel cup of coffee from the kitchen. He couldn't sleep anyway. Might as well go talk to Mom.

She was going to hear about this one way or the other. Better if the news came from him.

The sun was beginning to peek through the clouds when he pulled into the familiar drive in Baton Rouge. Mama's lilacs, bunched up next to the porch, filled the air with sweetness. He still recalled when Dad had teased her about planting them so close to the house, warning that a time would come when there would be no room to open the door. That time was fast approaching.

He rang the doorbell, not wanting to barge in and startle her. From inside the house barking erupted. Good old Nehemiah was on the job.

The lock clicked and the door scraped open, hanging a little. He needed to have a look at that.

"Ian!" Mom's face registered surprise and concern. "What are you doing here at this hour? Is something wrong?"

She shoved the glass door aside and plucked him into the living room. As always, his own face smiled out from every picture frame. Only this time, he was achingly aware that in none of the photos was he younger than five years old.

He wrapped his mother in a gentle bear hug and kissed the top of her head. "How ya doing?"

"Fit as a fiddle." She was still in her housecoat. Nehemiah bounced around her feet, grinning, tail wagging. "You hungry?"

He smiled. Mama was only happy when she was feeding someone. "Starved."

He followed her into the sunny kitchen where already the scent of coffee warmed the air. As a kid he'd loved this room with its delicious smells, warm colors and friendly chatter. He could still picture Dad sitting at the table with him as he struggled to understand math. He'd hated the subject. Only Dad's quiet, stubborn insistence that he do his best had gotten him through. They'd butted heads plenty over that. A spoiled kid. A strong, determined father. His throat filled with emotion at the memory.

Wryly, he considered how that dislike now haunted him. If he'd been better at math, maybe he would have paid more attention to the books at Isaiah House.

Mom opened the fridge and began dragging out various pancake makings. "You still haven't said what brings you up here today."

"Do I need a reason to visit my mom?" The word

sounded odd to him this morning, considering what he had to ask. But she was his mom in every way that counted.

"You do at seven in the morning. Have you even been to bed?"

"Don't fuss, Mama. I need to talk to you about something."

Spatula in hand, she turned from the sizzling pan of sausages. "That sounds important."

"It is." When she started to say more, he patted his belly and grinned. "But I want my breakfast first."

The old dog sidled up to his chair and Ian rubbed his ears. The liquid brown eyes adored him. He noticed the gray around the old setter's muzzle. "How old is Nehemiah now? Twelve? Thirteen?"

"Mmm. Let's see. You dragged him home from a football game one night. A ball of fluff that someone had dumped by the side of the road. I guess you were about sixteen. You were driving."

"He's old."

"Well, so am I. That's why the two of us do fine together." She blew on a link sausage until it cooled, then offered the meat to the dog. With an incongruent daintiness, the setter took the treat between his teeth and sauntered off.

"You'll never be old."

She flapped a hand at him and began dishing up the food. "I don't feel old but neither did your daddy."

"I still miss him."

"So do I. Every day. Sometimes I think I hear him out in that shop of his where the two of you built those birdhouses."

"And a lot of other things." The skills his dad had taught him had served him well in taking care of the aging mission house.

After pouring them both a cup of coffee, Mom set two filled plates on the round wooden table and sat down.

"You want some milk or juice with this?"

"Coffee's fine."

"All right then. Say grace and let's eat. I'm anxious to hear what's on your mind."

Ian offered a brief prayer for the food, but inside he prayed for wisdom and for his mother's health. The last thing he wanted to do was hurt her in any way. Whether she was his birth mother or not, she was everything a parent should be.

He poured a generous helping of maple syrup on his stack of pancakes and dug in.

"You make the best pancakes in Louisiana," he mumbled around an oversize bite.

She swatted his arm. "Don't talk with your mouth full."

They both chuckled at the familiar admonishment.

After a few rejuvenating minutes in which he polished off six pancakes and four sausages, he picked up his coffee and sat back with a replete sigh.

With eyes as blue as his, Margot studied him across her coffee mug. "What's troubling you, son?"

Where did he start? How did he begin to ask her if she'd lied to him all of his life?

"I had a visitor yesterday."

"Anyone I know?"

"I don't think so. He's from Oklahoma. A policeman. His name is Collin Grace."

Her cup clattered against the table. "Oklahoma?"

"I don't want to upset you, Mom. Forgive me if this hurts you in any way, but I have to know. Am I adopted?"

Her eyes flickered. She blinked several times, clearly distressed. Ian's stomach knotted. Please Lord, let her heart handle this.

Mom's fingers, thinned by age but still graceful, picked at a linen napkin. Ian's pulse accelerated with each blink of her eyes. He didn't want to hurt her. Not in a million years, but there were some things a man had to know.

"Mom, are you okay? Your heart—"

"My heart hurts, son, but not in the way you mean." She placed a hand atop his, the warm, mother love flowing out of her. "Maybe we should have told you before. I don't know. I never did know."

"So it's true?"

"Yes."

The word, though barely a whisper, boomed in his ears. He'd known, and yet the answer still startled him. Still shook him to the core.

"Who am I?"

"You're my son, Ian Robert Carpenter. The child your daddy and I couldn't conceive. The child God gave us. You will never know how long I prayed and mourned for a child."

"So you adopted me." Somehow saying the words made them real. He still couldn't quite take it in. Why had he not known? Why had he never guessed? The signs were there, but he'd never even looked at them until now.

"We'd almost given up on ever being parents, and

then the social worker called about you, a precious little boy, who was five years old and needed a family in a hurry. Daddy and I drove all night to get to you."

"Before you ever saw me?"

She nodded. "We knew you were ours the moment she called. Finally an answer to our prayers."

"Why don't I remember any of this?" Leaning forward, he steepled his hands together on the tabletop. "I was five. I should remember."

"Because you were sick, honey. By the time we arrived, you were in the hospital. Meningitis. The social worker had told us you weren't feeling well, but we had no idea how sick you were. As soon as I walked in that room and held you in my arms, I fell in love. I prayed so hard that God would spare you. He'd finally given us a child and you were at death's door."

"You adopted a sick kid with some kind of brain problem? Weren't you afraid of what you were getting?"

"Not once did we question if you were the right child. You were ours, sick or not. So sweet and kind-hearted. Even when the nurses had to poke you with IVs, you'd reassure them that it was okay even as tears ran down your face. How could we not fall in love with you?" She smiled, face full of memories. "We debated telling you. In fact, your daddy and I fought about the subject more than once."

"Dad wanted me to know."

"Yes. But you'd had such a hard start in life. The doctor said it was a mercy that you lost your memory, and I agreed. I wanted to protect you. To keep your sweet little nature free of the sad past. You deserved to have only good memories from that time forward. I didn't want you to remember the bad things."

But he had. Not consciously, but deep inside the recesses of his mind the past had lived on, tormenting him with dreams.

Part of him wanted to be angry with her, but he couldn't muster the strength. As she always had, Mama had done what she thought was best for him.

"What about my brothers? Why didn't you adopt them, too?"

Her face saddened. "No one told us about them, and we really didn't ask too many questions. All we knew was that you were a legal risk adoption from a very bad situation and that your birth mother was in the process of relinquishing rights. We were so wrapped up in caring for you we never considered that you might have siblings."

"How long have you known about them?"

"Since Christmas."

His mouth gaped, incredulous. "This past Christmas?"

"Please don't hate me, son. I couldn't bear to lose you."

Ian scooted back from the table and stood, gripping the top of the chair rail. "I could never hate you, Mom, but I am struggling to understand. It's a pretty big shock for a grown man to discover he doesn't know who he is."

"You are who you've always been. A good son, a wonderful man of God. This doesn't change who you are."

But it did. How could she not see that it did?

Mom came around the table to lay her hand on his heaving chest, soothing him as she'd done a hundred times before. "I mean it now. Don't go having an identity crisis. That's another reason I've kept quiet. You've always been sensitive."

Sensitive?

"You knew Collin was searching for me?"

"Back at Christmas he called, asking for you. Well, asking for Ian Grace who had been adopted from Oklahoma City." She turned away and started clearing the table. "I didn't believe him at first. So I put him off."

Ian could understand that. "I didn't believe him at first, either."

"Well, he's a persistent boy." Ian hid a smile at the gross misstatement. Collin had never been a boy. "He called again a month or so ago. This time before I could hang up, he said a couple of things that made me wonder if he could be telling the truth."

"So that's why you were acting so strange at Christmas. I thought you were sick and afraid to tell me."

"I'm sorry, son, I didn't know what to do when he called." She paused, his empty plate in her hand. "I love you so much. If I lost you…"

He'd expected to feel anger. Instead, love welled in him for this woman who had taken on a sick child, nurtured and loved and raised him to be a decent man. He'd come from the bottom, but the Carpenters' love hadn't allowed him to stay there.

"You could have told me." He took the plate from her hands, put it in the sink, then took her by the shoulders. Staring into the beloved face, lined now with years, he said, "I would have still been your baby boy. Nothing would have changed that."

Her lips trembled. Tears welled. "I know that now.

You are the man your daddy and I prayed you would be. You could have handled it."

Then she laid her head against his bursting chest and cried.

The drive back to New Orleans passed in a blur. Ian was tired. Shouldn't be driving, but he was far too emotional to sleep.

After the talk with Mom, he was ready to face Collin.

A brother. He could hardly take it in. He wondered what Gretchen would think. Would she consider him less than acceptable because of his tainted past? Or laugh at him for thinking such a thing?

Ah, what was he thinking? The relationship with Gretchen was over. She would never be able to trust anyone, certainly not him. And even if they could get past the argument over the mission, there was still her estrangement from the Lord. Funny how he'd let that slide of late, hoping she'd change for him.

He knew how foolish such thoughts were. A woman didn't change just because a man loved her. Tamma sure hadn't.

By the time he returned to the mission, he figured the place would be crawling with reporters. Even though he'd had no time or heart to watch the news last night the rumor of impropriety had to be everywhere today. Bad news traveled fast.

There was little he could do about that now, so for once, his family would come first. The mission could wait another day. Collin had been waiting for more than twenty years.

Even now, as he rode the Sheraton elevator to the fortieth floor, his big brother waited.

A service cart filled with towels and other assorted amenities rattled up as he stepped out. Though impatient to find room 4003, he held the door for the maid. Mama had taught him manners.

He rubbed a hand over his burning eyes. As hurt as he was to have been kept in the dark about something so vital, he owed his adoptive parents a lot.

The hotel security lock echoed in the hallway. Collin yanked open the door before Ian could knock.

"Hey." With the same probing intensity Ian noticed before, Collin motioned for him to enter. The guy must terrify suspects. "How are you?"

The question wasn't a nicety. He meant it.

"Better." Ian removed his cap and ran a hand through his hair. "Sorry to run out on you last night."

"No problem. Considering that you had no prior memory of me, who could blame you for being shocked? I was pretty shocked myself."

"You were?"

"I thought you were lying about the memory loss."

"I thought you were lying about being my brother, though I couldn't figure out why you'd do that."

"Anything else come back to you?"

"A lot of things." He pinched the ball cap into a V-shape. "I talked to my mother."

He didn't bother to correct the term. She was his mother.

"She told you."

"Everything she knew, which wasn't a lot. I was sick

when they first decided to adopt me. Some kind of amnesia brought on by the meningitis."

Collin nodded, quiet.

Ian studied the sculpted face, finding hints of the boy in the man. "You really are my brother."

"Yeah." Collin stuck his hands in his back pockets, movements stiff with tension.

His big brother was stressed to the max, and Ian wasn't sure how to go about easing the strain. They stood like what they were, two strangers grasping for something to say.

Emotions riotous, Ian longed to recapture all that was lost. For Collin, the feelings must be even more powerful.

Finally, the words threatening to choke him, Ian said, "Thanks for finding me. For all those years of searching. Thanks for not giving up."

Hope sprang into the man's dark eyes. "You mean that?"

"This may sound strange, but something in me always missed you."

Collin slowly removed his hands from his pockets. "I missed you, too."

They hovered there, inches apart. Ian wondered how Collin would react if he hugged him.

"Remember that bike we built out of parts from the dump?" he asked instead.

Collin's face softened. "You remember that?"

Ian grinned. "Yeah. And I also recall that you had a crush on some girl named Melinda."

Collin smirked. "Other way around. She had a crush on me."

"Yeah. Yeah. Tell it to someone who wasn't there."

Relief a palpable thing, Collin said, "You really do remember."

Ian grinned and clapped him on the shoulder. "I remember that you were the best brother anyone could ever have had."

Collin gazed at him, eyes bright. He cleared his throat. "You were, too."

"I was a pain."

"No, that was Drew."

They both chuckled then, lost in the memory of a childhood cut short.

"Tell me about Drew."

Collin's smile faded. "I wish I didn't have to."

"Is it bad?" Since the return of his memory, he'd imagined all kinds of possibilities for his wild brother, none of them good.

"The worst. Drew died in a fire when he was fifteen."

All the air went out of him. A brother gained. A brother lost. All in a matter of hours.

"Oh, man."

The room grew painfully silent while they both mourned the loss. The air-conditioning kicked on. In the next room someone ran water. Drew, the wild one, the fighter, was gone. Ian didn't recall much about him, but he remembered the brotherly love, the solid front they'd presented to the world. All for one. One for all. Now, he'd never have a chance to tell Drew how much that had meant to a scrawny little boy.

Thank you, Lord, for Collin. For at least sparing one.

Collin pulled a chair away from the built-in desk.

"Sit down, little brother, before you fall down. You look pretty weary."

"I didn't sleep much last night." To tell the truth, he was out on his feet.

"Wanna save this talk for another day?"

He shook his head. "No way. We have a lot of catching up to do. I'm not going anywhere."

Collin's stoic face bloomed into a smile. "I was hoping you'd say that. I bought some snacks, fruit, cheese, stuff like that." He motioned toward a large stash piled on the dresser. "Beats some of the things we've eaten."

Ian laughed and made himself comfortable. Collin had fed him as kid and now as an adult. Somehow that felt exactly right.

The rest of the afternoon flew by as the brothers caught up on twenty-three years. He learned that Collin had grown up in group homes, that he'd put himself through college, later becoming an Oklahoma City police officer. He learned of Collin's rescue farm for wounded animals and his love for a woman named Mia.

Pride surged through him. Collin, despite all the odds, had made a success of his life.

"Mia led me to the Lord," his brother said, dark eyes alight with the love he had for his fiancée. "And when I heard you were a minister, man, was I happy."

The comment was a reality check. Ian thumped the heels of both hands against his forehead. He'd been so engrossed in his personal situation for the last twenty-four hours that he'd shoved the mission's problems out of his thoughts.

"My days as a minister may be coming to a halt, at least here in New Orleans."

Collin popped a green grape in his mouth and chewed. "What does that mean?"

He told his brother about Gretchen's series, about the rumors and untrue allegations. He even told him about the situation with Roger, though he carefully refrained from using Roger's name.

"Last night, Channel Eleven aired a story about money embezzled from the mission with me as the prime suspect." He crushed a pop can with one hand and tossed it toward the trash can to join the other two he'd downed. "So, as Mama would say, the fat is about to hit the fire."

Collin shook his head. "Are you sure? I've sat in front of this tube all night and all day waiting for your call. I didn't see anything about your mission."

Ian sat up straighter. "Were you watching Channel Eleven? A gorgeous blonde with one of those short, flippy haircuts, huge green eyes and a voice that could melt a man's heart."

Collin lifted an eyebrow. "Is this a woman your brother should know about?"

"She would be. I wanted her to be."

"In love?"

"Yeah, but it's hopeless." In more ways than one.

"I watched her report last night. She's pretty, all right. But there was nothing on there about your mission."

Ian's heart did a *kerplunk*. "Seriously?"

"Not a word. She talked about some place that takes in recovering drug addicts."

"Second Chances?"

"I think that was it."

She'd told him about the place in glowing terms, holding it up as ideal.

Bewildered hope began to rise. "Not a word about Isaiah House?"

"My memory's not as bad as yours," Collin teased.

How could that be? Why wouldn't Gretchen follow through on her plans? She'd made a promise to the station. The segment was scheduled.

The ray of hope began to burn brighter in his tired spirit. Could she have decided to trust in him after all?

Chapter Seventeen

Car keys jangling, purse flapping against her side, Gretchen slogged into her apartment and collapsed in the nearest chair.

Last night she'd committed the reporter's cardinal sin. Today she'd paid for it.

To make matters worse, her heart hurt from the argument with Ian. He probably never wanted to see her again, especially after she'd embarrassed them both by calling him a liar and telling him she loved him all in one breath.

How messed up was that?

"Bad day at the office?" her roommate asked.

As usual Carlotta looked magnificent while Gretchen felt like an unmade bed. "You don't know the half of it."

"Kick off your shoes and relax. Tell Mama all about it."

"Mike threatened to fire me. Then he threatened to end the series. Then he told me to find him a good story and find it fast."

Carlotta munched the corner of a Fudgsicle. "What did you say to that?"

"I asked him if a certain reporter went berserk and killed her boss on the air, would that constitute a good story?"

Carlotta laughed and pointed the ice-cream bar. "I take it he was not amused."

"Who knows? I ducked out of there before the explosion."

"No regrets?" Carlotta knew what she'd decided.

"Are you kidding? My middle name is regrets." She shoved a hand through her hair, ripping through the gel that kept the side flip under control. "My whole life to this point has been regrettable. Until last night. Finally I did something right."

Carlotta rose and went into the kitchen. Her voice rose over the soft sucking noise of the refrigerator door being opened. "By killing the story on Ian?" She returned to the living room and handed Gretchen a fudge bar. "The things we do for love."

"Not only love, Carlotta. Oh, I'll admit that played a part." Okay, a huge part. Gretchen toed off her espadrilles and curled her feet beneath her, then unwrapped the cold treat. "But my decision was more about God, about doing what would please Him. After I prayed in the chapel, the choice was easy."

Carlotta held up one perfectly manicured hand. "You lost me there. I don't know much about religion."

"And I know too much. The point is God, not religion. Ian kept trying to tell me that, but I'm a hard head sometimes."

"Your boss would agree."

They both chuckled.

"What are you going to do about Ian?"

"I have no idea."

"The man should be groveling at your feet."

"I doubt if he even knows."

"Then tell him. You love him, don't you?"

Enough to risk her career for him. If Mike had his way, she'd be demoted a notch or two. Maybe even be phased out in the next round of changes. Double-crossing an obsessive boss wasn't the smartest career move. She licked her ice cream and fretted.

"Maybe you should give him a call."

"I doubt he'd want to talk to me. I called him a liar to his face." Worse than that, she'd said she loved him. "Besides I don't think Ian's interested in me that way."

"What! Girlfriend, are you smokin' crack? The man's nuts about you."

"Ian has a good heart. He cares about people, about their souls. That's probably all I mean to him. One more broken soul rescued."

"Oh, please. Give me a break here. I think I'm going to throw up." She stormed over and yanked Gretchen's Fudgsicle away.

"Hey, give that back!"

"Not until you wake up. Love doesn't come along very often. I'm your best friend and I won't let you blow this chance. Ian's a keeper."

"Yeah. He's everybody's keeper." She grabbed for the Fudgsicle but Carlotta was too fast for her.

"Do you love him or not?" She waggled the ice cream just out of reach. "Admit it."

"I told you I do." She reached for the bar.

"I can't hear you." Carlotta taunted.

Her voice rose a notch. "I love him."

"Louder."

Leave it to Carlotta to tease her into feeling better. Gretchen bounced up, standing on the chair to shout, "I am crazy in love with Ian Carpenter!"

Though she had no idea what to do about it.

A nanosecond later the doorbell rang. Wearing a smirk, Carlotta returned the Fudgsicle and went to answer.

One peek through the security window and she burst into laughter. "Why don't you scream that again right now?"

Gretchen's heart slammed against her rib cage. "Why?"

"Because there is a very handsome, rather harried-looking preacher standing on our front porch."

"Oh, no." She slithered into the chair. Had Ian heard her yelling like a deranged baboon?

"Oh, yes."

She looked a mess. Her hair was sticking up all over the place. Her makeup had long since melted away. And she probably had chocolate on her face from the tussle with Carlotta.

Nevertheless, her roommate opened the door.

Without a word, Ian marched right in.

He looked wonderful.

"You look exhausted."

With a grin as wide as the Mississippi, Carlotta edged

around the two. She pumped knowing eyebrows at Gretchen. "Want a fudge bar, Ian?"

"No."

A fudge bar was the last thing on his mind. All he could think about was Gretchen. If Collin was right, she had risked her job for him. And he needed to know why. What changed her mind?

Carlotta snickered. "Want me to get lost for an hour or two?"

At the risk of being rude, he shot her a glance. "Would you?"

Her response was another laugh. Any other time, he would have wondered about Carlotta's behavior. Today, all he could think about was Gretchen. A ridiculous hope beat inside his weary chest. Although her decision may not have a thing to do with him, a fool could always hope. She *had* said she loved him.

"Cool. I'm gone." Carlotta grabbed her purse, jangled her keys and disappeared. Ian hardly noticed when the door snapped shut.

Gretchen sat in a big stuffed chair, eyes wide and greener than spring, a fudge bar dripping onto her fingers. He had never seen her this quiet.

He stood over her, hands on hips. "What happened to the story?"

She licked her lips. Chocolate stained one spot. "I killed it."

"Why?"

"For a lot of reasons. But mostly because, last night, I woke up." The threat of tears deepened her eyes to moss. He wanted to yank her into his arms and kiss her and proclaim his love. But he couldn't, and the pain of holding such a beautiful thing inside was almost too much to bear.

"Woke up from what?"

"What you said really got to me. When I walked out of your room, I was so confused. I stopped in the chapel to think. The next thing I knew, I was praying."

He needed so badly to touch her. This time he didn't refrain. Pulse thundering, he knelt in front of her and gently took her hand. "You prayed?"

Gretchen nodded, tears glistening. "You were right all along. I didn't realize it, but I've blamed God for what happened to me as a teenager. After I started reading the Gospels—"

"You didn't tell me that."

"I had to be sure for myself this time. I couldn't take a chance on being fooled again."

"And?" Ian thought he would explode from the anticipation.

"Last night, everything came together. I recognized the truth I've always searched for. Not the truth of a reporter's facts, but a greater reality. The one in here." She touched her heart. "A wicked man hurt me and Maddy, not God. He gave his Son for me. And now that I've let Him into my life, I'm free for the first time since my parents joined the commune."

He'd come here for some answers about the story and to thank her. Never in his wildest hopes had he imagined anything this wonderful.

"I think you just made me the happiest man in the world."

She blinked at him, puzzled. "Yeah?"

"Yeah." With exquisite care, Ian wiped a tear from her cheekbone. "But I don't understand what this has to do with killing the story."

A tremulous smile touched her mouth. "You asked me to trust you. I couldn't. Not until I trusted God. Then I was able to see that your life and your work speak the truth. You don't have to say a word. I've watched you. I've seen your integrity. If you ask me for time to work something out, I have to believe there is a good reason."

Roger. Ian bit down on his jaw to keep the secret inside him. "There is."

She touched his cheek. "I know."

It felt so good to hear her say that.

Heart pounding, hope soaring, he took the melting ice cream and tossed it into a nearby wastebasket. Then, slowly, very slowly, he pulled her hand to his lips and tasted the sticky chocolate.

"I love you, Gretchen. I have for a long time."

The threatening tears fell in earnest now. "I love you, too."

From his knees, Ian gave a tug, gently bringing her to the floor in front of him. They were face-to-face, heart-to-heart. "I've wanted to do this for a very long time."

With pure joy, he bracketed her delicate face, sliding fingers into her hair as he stared into the deep green eyes of a soul he loved. And then, with a thankful, trembling sigh, he kissed her.

Her mouth tasted of cold chocolate and warm love, its velvet sweetness a reward for months of self-denial. When he lifted his head, her smile greeted him.

"I love you, Ian. So much."

Though he wanted nothing to spoil this moment, he also wanted no secrets between them. If they were to have the relationship he longed for, he wanted to begin with honesty.

"You may not feel that way after I tell you something." Not every woman wanted a man from a tainted past.

"Nothing you say is going to change how I feel. Not now."

"I need to tell you anyway. Open and honest. Love accepts nothing less." He played with her fingers, raising and lowering them. "You told me about your childhood. There's something you need to know about mine."

A small frown of curiosity formed between her eyebrows. "You sound so serious. Is it bad?"

"I'll let you decide." Ian leaned his back against the padded chair and drew Gretchen into the shelter of his side. If she rejected him now, he wasn't sure what he would do. "Remember when I told you that I have a brother?"

"The man at the restaurant?"

He nodded. "Collin Grace."

"I didn't believe you. I thought you were trying to distract me from discovering the real reason for that clandestine meeting."

No surprise there. "Collin *is* my brother, Gretchen, but I didn't know until the night at the Treehouse. We were separated as boys by foster care. I was adopted. He wasn't."

Over the next few minutes, Ian shared the story of his broken childhood, of the amnesia and of Collin's relentless search, praying all the while that she wouldn't think less of him afterward.

"So," he said at the end, "I'm not the man you always thought I was. I'm the product of a dysfunctional, drug-addicted mess. And if that changes your feelings, I'll understand."

She twisted around to stare at him. "Are you nuts?"

"Why?"

"You think your childhood is crazier than mine? That it changes you somehow to be adopted? Come on, Ian. Get real."

"You don't mind?"

"You silly, adorable man." She kissed his cheek. "A smart preacher once told me that we are the sum total of our past experiences. They either make us or break us. The choice is ours."

"Did I say that?"

"Mmm-hmm. You're right, too. Where you come from, both as a birth child and as an adopted son, make you the incredible man of God you are today. The man I love with all my heart."

Overjoyed, he pulled her close. "Seriously?"

"If I thought your childhood damaged you or changed you in some way, I wouldn't want to marry you so much."

A beat passed as her words soaked in. "That sounded a little like a proposal."

Her voice held wonder. "I think it was."

Ian laughed, the joy bubbled up in him like a fountain. "Then I accept." He reached for her. "Come here, woman, I want to taste that chocolate ice cream again."

And he did.

After a long kiss that left them both smiling and a little starry-eyed, Gretchen leaned her head on his shoulder and said, "I can't remember ever being this happy."

"Me, too." Yesterday he'd thought his life's work was in jeopardy and that he and Gretchen were finished for good. Today he held the woman of his dreams in his arms and though the problems at the mission weren't resolved by any means, Gretchen had given him time to work them out.

She'd sacrificed her credibility to save his.

"Wait a minute," he said, as the thought took root. "I just realized something. Are you in trouble at the station?"

"A little, but don't worry." She pushed at a wildly out-of-control lock of hair. "If I can find another good story right away, and get some decent viewer response, I'll be okay."

"You'll have the mission story soon, and even though I'd rather it never aired, it's going to be news. Might as well be you doing the story. At least I know you'll be fair to—"

He caught himself in time not to say Roger's name. His bookkeeper had promised to go public about the missing money as soon as his son was in the custody of border police in Texas. Until then, Ian's lips were sealed.

"I appreciate that, Ian. I really do, but I need something right away. The kind of story that will grab viewers. You know, a shocker or a tearjerker." She scratched at her neck and tried to look innocent. "I don't suppose you'd let some of the kids at the mission tell their stories?"

"Not a chance."

"Didn't think so," she said agreeably.

An idea niggled at Ian's brain. "I have a thought that might work."

"At this point, I'm interested in anything."

"What about a reunion story? Two brothers. A sick little boy with amnesia. A key chain they both carried for more than twenty years."

She stilled. Excitement animated her expression. "Are you serious? Would you mind?"

Happiness expanded Ian's chest. At last, something he could give her. "I'd have to ask Collin. He's a pretty private guy. But I think he'll agree."

"Oh, Ian," she threw herself against his chest, propelling him backward against the stuffed chair. "I could kiss you for this."

Ian laughed. "That's another thing I can help you with." And then his lips met hers.

Epilogue

Spring fragranced the air the day Ian's big brother, Collin, returned to Louisiana, this time bringing his fiancée, Mia Carano. With her warm, effervescent personality and a smile that could melt an iceberg, Mia was the perfect compliment to Collin's intensity. Ian liked her on sight.

Mama, of course, had insisted on a family get-together. So the clan gathered, Collin and Mia, Ian and Gretchen, along with Mama in Baton Rouge. Ian felt a pride he'd never imagined. His family. All of them together.

From the expression on Collin's face, he enjoyed the situation just as much. After a hilarious round of golf, the foursome had returned to Mama's house for Creole chicken.

Now they all sat in the living room, surrounded by Ian's trophies, for which he took considerable good-natured ribbing from his big brother. Even though he laughed, Ian had a fleeting sense of sadness. Neither

Collin nor Drew even had the privilege of a mother's doting adoration. He was indeed a blessed man.

The television, though muted, flickered scenes from CNN while they talked. Mama, in her element, bustled around filling glasses with sweet tea and offering more cookies than anyone could ever eat. To his relief, a single medication had solved the problem of her arrhythmia and she was back at the club, swimming every day and, as she put it, "Taking care of the old people."

They were discussing Gretchen's story on their reunion.

"How did it go?" Collin asked. He'd left Louisiana before the piece aired.

"I brought a copy for you. We can watch it later if you'd like. Either way, the DVD is yours to keep. Viewers loved it."

"What about the other situation?" Collin looked from Ian to Gretchen.

"I told her everything," Ian said. "My bookkeeper turned himself in the day after you went back to Oklahoma." Channel Eleven had filmed the exclusive story on that, too, complete with Roger's desperate attempt to help his troubled son, now in jail in Texas.

"What will happen to him?"

"Our lawyers are pushing for restitution instead of jail time. Given the circumstances, I think he'll get it. At least that's what I'm praying for."

"No animosity for the bad publicity? For letting you take the blame?"

"Roger's a good man who made a bad choice." He

didn't like talking about this. He was no saint himself and the mission would recover from the negative publicity. Even though the audit reported the shortfall, no other discrepancies were found. As a result donors were calling with both financial and moral support. "Do you mind if we change the subject? Gretchen and I have an announcement to make."

He'd been waiting for the perfect time, and what better time than now when all his family was together.

His mother's hands flew to her lips. "Oh, I knew it."

Everyone laughed.

Ian cleared his throat, nervous, but excited, too. He reached into his pocket and took out the ring box secreted there this morning.

Gretchen gasped, hands fluttering to her surprised mouth "Ian. You didn't warn me."

"Wouldn't be a surprise if I did." He slipped to one knee. "I wanted to do this right, in front of the people I love most." He glanced from Collin to his mother. "And those who love me most."

For it was true. His mother loved him enough to want to protect him. His brother loved him enough to never give up on finding him.

His throat filled. Struggling to stay composed, he took Gretchen's small hand in his. She trembled and he almost forgot the carefully prepared speech that he'd practiced all day.

"Gretchen, I love you. You know that. You also know I want to share my life with you." He slid the simple diamond onto her finger. "I can't promise you riches or perfection, but with God as our guide, I can promise to love and cherish you all the days of my life. Will you marry me?"

She gently caressed the side of his face. "You know I will."

Ian stood and pulled her up. The room around them had gone dead silent except for the sound of his mother's sniffling. When he kissed her, everyone erupted into applause.

When the kiss ended he smiled tenderly into Gretchen's eyes, and then turned to his brother. "Collin, would you be my best man?"

His brother's face glowed with unspoken emotion. He stood and offered his hand. "I'd be honored."

Then to Ian's great joy Collin engulfed him in a brotherly hug.

During the next few minutes, a good kind of chaos reigned as they answered questions and made plans.

Suddenly in the midst of everything, Mia leaped from her chair and rushed to the television set. "Shh. Everybody hush." She pushed the volume button. "It's Collin and Ian."

"Oh, my goodness." Gretchen stopped admiring her ring. "That's CNN." She squealed. "Ian, CNN picked up our story."

Sure enough, Gretchen's sensitive portrayal played across the screen.

"A brother's bond," she said, her professional voice tender and ripe with feeling. "The undying love that kept Collin Grace searching for his younger brothers for more than twenty years."

The piece moved on, sensitive but revealing and highly

emotional, including the sad fact that one brother, Drew, had died in a fire at age fifteen. The photojournalist had done a beautiful job of editing, fading from the old photo of the three of them to the men they were today.

Ian glanced at Collin, saw the hidden emotion. Tears ran down Mia's face as she gripped her fiancé's hand tight enough to turn her knuckles white. Even though he'd watched the film a dozen times with Gretchen, his own throat filled.

As the feature moved toward a conclusion the camera focused on a pair of masculine hands. Each held an identical ichthus.

Gretchen's silky smooth voice said, "Separated as boys, reunited as men. Connected by one brother's memory and the Christian symbol that each carried in his pocket. Coincidence? Or divine intervention?"

The camera lens slowly closed, spotlighting the Jesus fish until the picture faded to black and returned to the CNN anchor.

"What beautiful work, Gretchen," Mia said, drying her eyes. She reached for the DVD Gretchen had given Collin. "We'll treasure this forever."

"So will I," Gretchen said.

"So will we all." Margot crossed the room and placed a hand on Collin's shoulder. "I wish I would have known. I always wanted another son."

Awash in emotions, Ian was relieved to hear the chirp of Gretchen's cell phone. She glanced at the caller ID. "No escape from work."

"Probably calling to congratulate you. It's not every day you get national exposure."

She pressed the phone to her ear.

"Are you serious?" Her eyes flashed to Ian. "That's awesome. Did you get the number?" She motioned for a pen. Ian grabbed a pad and pencil from Mom's end table. After scribbling something, Gretchen said, "You have no idea. Thanks."

She ended the call but stood staring at the tiny phone, stunned by something.

"What's up?" Ian asked.

"Someone who saw the CNN report called the station." She looked from Ian to Collin. "You're not going to believe this."

She had their full attention now.

"What is it? What's going on?" Ian saw the mix of concern and excitement on her face.

"I'm almost afraid to tell you. Afraid to get your hopes up. But this could be incredible news."

The room pulsated with her tension. Whatever the caller had said must be good.

Finally, Gretchen took a deep breath and blurted, "According to the caller, your brother Drew may still be alive."

* * * * *

Dear Reader,

This series, THE BROTHERS' BOND, is truly a labor of love for me. Throughout scripture the Christian is commanded to care for the needy. Ian took this command to heart when he opened Isaiah House. When I began to study Isaiah 58 and Matthew 25, Ian's life verses, I became convinced of my own lacking in this area. Orphan children especially are helpless without our compassion. The number of parentless children worldwide is staggering—in the multimillions. Here in America we have social orphans, like the Grace brothers in this series, estimated at more than half a million. It breaks my heart and moves me to action.

No one can help them all, but each of us can do something.

Thank you for reading *A Touch of Grace.* As always I enjoy hearing from readers and value your thoughts on my stories. You may contact me at www.lindagoodnight.com or at Linda Goodnight, c/o Steeple Hill Books, 233 Broadway Suite 1001, New York, NY 10279.

Blessings to you,

Linda Goodnight

QUESTIONS FOR DISCUSSION

1. Ian's shoe purchases are a symbol in the story. Why is he compelled to buy shoes? What kind of events precede each new purchase?

2. Ian's recurring nightmare is the key to the childhood he can't remember. Do you believe that the subconscious mind tries to tell us things through dreams? Have you ever had a recurring dream? What does scripture say about dreams?

3. Ian feels driven to help the needy, even to the point of exhaustion. Was his ministry a psychological need to rectify his childhood? Or a true calling from God in his life?

4. Gretchen blames God for the abuse she experienced as a child. Was God responsible? Why or why not?

5. What does Jesus say about religious leaders who distort scripture for their own purposes? Does this still happen today? Can you give examples?

6. Ian tells Gretchen that she should study the Bible for herself. Is this important? Why? Have you ever studied scripture and discovered you had been wrongly taught?

7. Ian is shocked to discover that he is adopted. Should adopted children be told? How do you feel about closed adoptions? Would you adopt a child if you thought the birth mother might come back and try to regain custody?

8. Many children end up in foster care and many more languish in orphanages around the world. What is a Christian's responsibility to orphans? See if you can find scripture references to support your answer. Are today's churches following the call of Christ to the orphans?
9. Ian made a decision to conceal Roger's crime. Does he do the right thing? How would you have handled the situation?
10. At the conclusion of the book, Gretchen asks if the brothers' reunion is coincidence or divine intervention. Which do you think it is? Do you believe God intervenes this way in people's lives?